Where Wildflowers Bloom

FRUIT PRESS

Copyright © 2026 by Hailey Renee

All rights reserved.

No part of this book may be reproduced in any form or by any electronic or mechanical means, including information storage and retrieval systems, without written permission from the author, except for the use of brief quotations in a book review.

No part of this book may be used or reproduced in any manner for the purpose of training artificial intelligence technologies or systems.

Cover by Brittany Padgett

❀ Formatted with Vellum

Where Wildflowers Bloom

HAILEY RENEE

For those who feel most alive where the wildflowers grow.

A Very Many Blooms Ago

Fifty years ago, the mountains were wilder. They weren't the carefully tended, sun-drenched slopes you see now. They were a tangle of stubborn saplings, gnarly roots, and earth that refused to yield without a fight. The air was sharp and alive, carrying the scent of pine and the tang of creek water that cut through the hollows like a silver thread.

Henry and Clara hadn't expected it to be easy. They were young, headstrong, full of that reckless certainty that only comes before the years make you wiser. Henry had grown up in the nearby town, son of a modest blacksmith, used to hard labor and the smell of coal dust in his hair. Clara had grown up in the city but dreamed of a quieter life, where soil could get under her nails, her sunhat would not be big enough for her teeming mind, and birdsong was the morning alarm.

Henry drove the old truck up the winding dirt road, Clara perched on the passenger seat with a notebook balanced on her knees, scribbling down wild ideas about flower beds, orchard rows, and wandering trails. The place smelled like wilderness, alive with wet moss, rotting leaves, and the faint, stubborn perfume of flowers that had refused to be tamed for decades.

"We can do this," Clara said, her eyes sparkling with more hope than reality warranted.

Henry chuckled, patting the steering wheel. "We'll do it, or we'll die trying."

The first year was a symphony of errors. The trees they planted leaned drunkenly in the wind, their roots half-exposed. The first greenhouse Clara tried to build collapsed under a mid-April snowstorm. Henry lost count of how many chicken houses he rebuilt after they were overturned by raccoons—or, in one memorable night, by their overly ambitious goats. Seeds went missing. Soil was stolen by erosion, and half of the land was more mud than roots.

Clara cried once, standing knee-deep in the greenhouse rubble, hands covered in dirt and tears, convinced they were cursed. But Henry didn't let her see him falter. He simply put a muddy hand on her shoulder, knelt down so they were eye to eye, and said, "We'll figure it out. Together. Always together."

And somehow, they did. Slowly, painfully, the earth began to bend to their will. Saplings took root. Greenhouses stood straight. Chickens clucked where they were supposed to, and the goats . . . well, the goats learned some boundaries. They worked sunrise to sunset, often arguing over trivialities— whether the east meadow should be for wildflowers or vegetables, which trail to cut first, who could coax the stubborn soil into submission—but always ending with shared laughter, a squeeze of the hand, or a shared bottle of sweet tea on the porch at dusk.

It was during one of those late afternoons, as the sun burned low behind the peaks, that Henry realized something. Clara had been dreaming aloud again, muttering about wildflowers that grew like they had a mind of their own, beds that curved and flowed with the land instead of against it, trails that wound through the property and disappeared into the trees. He'd been silent, observing her—her hair catching in the sunlight, her cheeks flushed with excitement, her hands moving in tiny gestures as she painted the vision with words.

Henry didn't say anything at first. He went into the shed, rifled through scrap wood and tools, and got to work. For hours, he measured and sawed, hammered and sanded, sometimes talking to himself, sometimes laughing at the ridiculousness of the project. When he finally came out, sweat-drenched and smeared with sawdust, he carried a wooden sign. Simple, unpainted at first, but strong. He brushed the dust off the surface, wiped his hands on his shirt, and called Clara over.

"What's that?" she asked, eyebrows raised.

Henry didn't answer. He just held it out. And as she took it in her hands, reading the carved letters—*Where Wildflowers Bloom*—her breath caught.

"You made this . . . for me?" she whispered, meeting his gaze. The corners of his mouth lifted in a grin, just the tiniest one, the one that said more than words ever could.

"I did," he said, voice steady, but soft. "Because wherever we go from here, I want you to remember, this is ours. All of it. Every misstep, every mess, every bloom that fights to grow."

She looked at the sign again, then at him, and laughed through tears, that mix of joy and disbelief that comes only with the deepest happiness. She hugged him fiercely, hands still clutching the wood, and for a long moment, the chaos of the farm—the muddy boots, the stubborn saplings, the crooked fences—mattered so little it almost didn't exist.

That was the beginning. Trails were cut and recut. Flower beds were planted, ripped out, replanted. Crops failed and thrived. Chickens and goats ran amok more often than not. And yet, year after year, they persisted. Their love grew alongside the land, sometimes stubborn, sometimes quiet, sometimes overwhelming, but always there—rooted and blooming in tandem with the farm.

Every spring, they'd repaint the *Where Wildflowers Bloom* sign, bright and cheerful, a little more worn each year but a symbol of persistence, hope, and devotion. And every spring, Clara would marvel at the resilience of the flowers—and of Henry—and smile, knowing they had built something more than a farm. They had built a life.

By the time the sun set on that first long summer, the air heavy with the scent of fresh-turned earth and early blooms, the farm was messy, beautiful, and theirs. And in the quiet moments, when they would sit side by side on the porch, sipping lukewarm tea, watching the chickens chase the last slivers of sunlight, Henry would squeeze her hand, and they would both know. They had planted more than just seeds. They had planted a life where love—and wildflowers—could grow.

Hazel

A RUSTIC WELCOME

The scent of rich earth and wildflowers hangs in the air as I pull into Maple Hollow, the little Appalachian town I now call home. A warm golden hue settles over the rolling hills, while a crisp late-summer breeze stirs the leaves along the two-lane road. It's picturesque in a way that feels like something out of a storybook. Peaceful. A fresh start.

Pine & Petal appears at the end of the gravel driveway, its weathered wooden sign swaying slightly in the breeze. The farmhouse is small but charming, its white paint peeling in places, the wraparound porch inviting despite its age. Beyond it, rows of overgrown flower beds stretch toward the tree line, tangled with weeds and the remnants of last season's blooms. It's mine now. *All of it.*

I kill the engine and sit there for a moment, gripping the steering wheel with clammy hands. This is it. No turning back now.

Three weeks ago, I was wearing heels that pinched my feet, trapped in a gray office cubicle, seeing my dream of doing something meaningful slip further away with every endless meeting. I spent years climbing the corporate ladder, earning a business degree, making my parents proud—but I was miserable.

When my high school sweetheart relationship ended in spectacular, heart-wrenching flames, I realized I had nothing tying me to that life anymore.

So I quit my job, drained a portion of my savings, and bought a flower farm from a sweet elderly couple looking to retire in Florida. A reckless decision? Probably. But standing here, surrounded by the crisp mountain air and the promise of something new, I can't bring myself to regret it.

I climb out of the truck and stretch, rolling my shoulders as I take in the property. It needs work, so much work, but I can already picture what it could be. Rows of vibrant dahlias and snapdragons, a greenhouse bursting with life, fresh bouquets wrapped in twine, ready for the local market.

My pulse skitters between excitement and absolute terror. Because, truthfully, I have no idea what I'm doing. I don't have farming experience. I've never run a business on my own. Hell, I don't even know how to use the equipment the Marshalls left behind. But I'm stubborn, and if there's one thing I refuse to do, it's fail.

A deep voice cuts through my thoughts.

"You're the one who bought the place?"

I turn to find a man standing at the edge of the property, arms crossed. He's tall, broad-shouldered, and looks like he was carved straight out of the mountains—rugged, weathered, and entirely unimpressed. A layer of dirt clings to his work-worn jeans, and his flannel sleeves are rolled up, revealing tanned forearms that speak of long hours in the sun. His dark hair is tousled, his jaw shadowed with scruff. And his scowl? It could curdle fresh milk.

"That's me." I lift my chin, forcing a polite smile. "Hazel Huntington."

His gaze flicks over me, from my clean jeans and brand-new work boots to the way I'm standing awkwardly next to my truck like I have no idea what I'm doing. Which, fair. I don't.

"Huh." He exhales sharply, shaking his head. "Should've figured."

My brows knit together. "Figured what?"

"That you're not a farmer."

I bristle. "I could be."

He snorts. "Not likely."

"And you are?"

"Beau Rosewood." He jerks a thumb toward the property next door. "I run Rosewood Orchards."

Of course. I'd heard about the orchard—and a few *other* things—from the Marshalls, one of the biggest apple farms in the area. That explains the lingering scent of apples on the wind and crates stacked in the distance.

"Well, Beau," I say, trying to keep my tone light despite the way he's looking at me, "it's nice to meet you."

He doesn't return the sentiment. Instead, he sighs, rubbing a hand over his face like this is already exhausting him. "Look, I don't care what you do with the place, but keep your mess on your side of the fence."

My mouth falls open. "Excuse me?"

"You're gonna realize real quick that running a flower farm isn't some romantic little dream," he says gruffly. "It's work. Hard work. And if you can't hack it, don't expect anyone else to clean up the disaster."

Anger flares. "I'm not looking for a handout, thanks."

His gaze narrows. "Good."

And with that, he walks away, back toward his orchard, leaving me standing there, seething.

So much for a warm welcome.

My phone starts buzzing against my hip like an angry wasp. I grumble, already knowing who it is before I even fish it out. Sure enough, the screen is lit up with a string of frazzled texts and missed calls from the same name.

Just as I'm about to lock the screen and ignore it, another call comes through. The persistent chime echoes through the quiet fields.

I press accept and put on my best "fancy" voice, the one I used to use in meetings when I had to pretend I cared.

"Hello?" I say firmly.

"Hazel! Where are you?!" Ruby's frantic voice bursts through the speaker, breathless and panicked, like she's been running in circles. Knowing her, she probably has. "Do you have any idea how much of a disaster today has been? The quarterly report is due, Mr. Lancaster is breathing down my neck, and someone put decaf in the espresso machine—DECAF, HAZEL. We are in a state of emergency."

I pinch the bridge of my nose, willing patience into my voice. "Ruby, I told you—multiple times. Four, to be exact. I quit. I gave you my two weeks' notice, and you can handle this."

Silence. A sharp inhale. Then a small, pitiful huff. "I miss you," she whispers.

The knot of frustration in my body loosens just a little. Ruby was the only person I'd miss from that awful office—the only part of that life that made the endless spreadsheets and mind-numbing meetings bearable.

My voice softens. "I miss you too."

"Fine." She sniffles, then, with a dramatic flair, "Go live your little farm life. But if I die from corporate stress, just know I'm haunting you."

"I'd expect nothing less." A laugh bubbles up, surprisingly.

"Good. Now, I have to go deal with this caffeine catastrophe before there's a full-blown mutiny. Liam is already moving into your office. But hey, if you ever decide you hate flowers and want to drown in data entry again, just know I'll be waiting."

"Not happening," I say, smiling. Ignoring the comment about the dingbat that broke my heart.

"We'll see," she hums, unconvinced.

I end the call and stare at the phone for a moment, a strange mix of emotions swirling. Then I tuck it back into my pocket, straighten my shoulders, and take a deep breath of fresh mountain air.

I made the right choice. Even if a certain grumpy neighbor and everyone else think otherwise.

I face the farmhouse, my new home.

The porch railing looks like it's seen better days, and a single shutter hangs slightly crooked, but despite all of that, warmth radiates from the place. It's lived in. Loved. And now, it's mine. I don't know how many times I have to say that for it to feel real, but . . . I don't care. I really *did it.*

The thought sends a rush of nervous excitement through me.

I grab my keys and head up the creaking wooden steps, my boots scuffing against the worn boards. The screen door screeches when I pull it open, and the front door sticks for a second before giving way with a soft *whoosh* of air, like the house is exhaling its first breath in my presence.

Stepping inside, I'm hit with the scent of aged wood, faint lavender, and something floral—maybe remnants of whatever candles the Marshalls used before they packed up and left. Sunlight streams in through lace-curtained windows, illuminating dust motes that swirl lazily in the air.

The living room is cozy, though a little outdated. A floral-patterned couch sits against one wall, a hand-stitched quilt draped over the back. A coffee table, scarred with years of use, sits in the center of the room, and built-in shelves line the far wall, some still holding a few forgotten knick-knacks—a ceramic bird, a faded photo frame, a large handmade wooden sign that reads: *Where Wildflowers Bloom.*

I set my bag down and run a hand over the worn surface of the kitchen counter as I pass through. The farmhouse sink is deep, the cabinets old but sturdy. The appliances are a mix of vintage and modern—functional, if not entirely fashionable.

It's not sleek or polished like my old apartment in the city. There are no marble countertops, no stainless-steel appliances, no perfectly curated decor. But it's real. It has *heart*.

I wander down the hallway, peeking into rooms as I go. The first is a small office with a sun-warmed desk and a window that overlooks the flower fields. The next is a guest room, its bed covered in an old-fashioned patchwork quilt. And finally, my room.

It's simple, with a four-poster bed, a weathered dresser, and windows that let in the golden afternoon light. I step inside, trailing my fingers over the edge of the bedframe.

I sink onto the edge of the bed and exhale. It's terrifying stepping into the unknown like this. I breathe in the peaceful silence as I stand and walk over to the window, eager to take in the view of my new kingdom. Pulling back the curtain, the sight that greets me leaves me momentarily breathless.

The flower fields stretch out like a patchwork quilt, but that isn't what caught my eye. It's the large, weathered barn that looms just beyond my property line, its red paint fading. I move closer to the glass, curiosity piqued. And that's when I see him.

Beau Rosewood, in all his rugged glory, is standing just outside the barn, a sharpening tool in his hand. He's focused, muscles flexing as he works, oblivious to my gaze. But then he looks up, and our eyes lock.

Our properties are close. Too close. There's no thick stand of trees between us, no stone wall or hedgerow. Just a narrow gravel strip—technically a shared right-of-way—and a waist-high fence made of split rails and rusted wire that sags in places like it's tired of standing between us.

My heart races, a sudden flush creeping up my cheeks as I realize he sees me. Vulnerability washes over me, and instinctively, I pull back from the window, hoping the curtain will conceal me from his view. *What am I doing? This is ridiculous.*

But something is unnerving about the way he looks at me. His brow furrows, and those piercing eyes seem to weigh my every move. For a moment, the world outside falls away, and it's just the two of us, suspended in this strange connection.

Then I remember that I'm peering at him from my bedroom window, and the warmth in my cheeks deepens. *What must he think of me?*

I step back until I'm against the wall, my heart thudding. This is just one more complication I didn't sign up for, a grumpy neighbor who looks like he stepped out of a rugged romance novel, sharpening tools while I sit here feeling exposed and foolish.

I take a deep breath, trying to steady myself. This is my home now. I'm not going to let a brooding neighbor throw me off my game.

With newfound determination, I shake off the lingering embarrassment and head back to the kitchen, ready to hopefully mark off some of my to-do list before night rolls in. I can handle a flower farm, and I can definitely handle a stubborn neighbor. *Right?*

I can hear the faint sound of metal scraping against metal as Beau sharpens his tools. I glance out the window one last time, but he's focused on his work, and I can't help but wonder what it is about him that feels so unsettling yet intriguing.

I shake my head, turning my focus back to the tasks ahead. This place won't fix itself.

Tying up my hair with a pencil from the kitchen counter, I pull on a pair of cleaning gloves that are two sizes too big, and crank up a playlist I've used for everything from finals week to post-breakup deep cleans. Hazel's war mode: activated.

By late evening, I've managed to scrub two cabinets,

unearth a very suspicious tin of cinnamon from the 80s, and accidentally scare a mouse out of the mudroom. There's a pile of donation-bound "what even is this?" objects forming by the front door, and my shirt is streaked with bleach from an unfortunate spray bottle incident. But the place feels a little less forgotten now. However, nowhere near finished.

I stand in the middle of the living room with my hands on my hips, sweat glistening at my temples, surveying the chaos around me.

"Well," I murmur to the crooked lamp in the corner, "we're a long way from PinBoard-ready, but at least you're no longer haunted-looking."

The lamp, of course, doesn't answer. Which is probably for the best. If it did, I'd already be halfway back to Washington.

I laugh, sharp and a little delirious, as I do a mock bow to the empty room. "Thank you, thank you. Tonight's performance of *One Woman Against Dust Bunnies* was brought to you by too much caffeine and questionable life choices."

I shake my head at myself, grinning despite the ache in my back, and decide that's enough for one day. The boxes can wait, the weeds outside can wait, even the suspicious cinnamon can wait. Tonight, I'm claiming victory.

In the bedroom, I unroll my sleeping bag on the four-poster bed, the mattress too musty to trust just yet. The walls creak with every step, like the house itself is settling into the fact that someone new is here.

I crawl inside the bag, tugging it up to my chin, and stare at the ceiling beams stretching into shadow.

It's so quiet. Too quiet. The kind of quiet that makes you suddenly aware of your own heartbeat, of how far away you are from anyone else. No car headlights sweeping across the walls. Just darkness pressing in at the windows and the sound of crickets far off in the fields.

I exhale, slow and shaky. "Okay," I whisper into the dark, as if the house is listening. "We've got this. You and me."

But as the wind stirs through the cracks and the barn creaks in the distance, I can't help but wonder just how much *this* really is.

PAGES & DUST

The bell above Cedar & Sage Books jingles as I push the door open. The shop is smaller than I expected, the kind of place where every inch of wall is packed with shelves and little nooks of things people have left behind or donated. There are stacks of old cookbooks, a jar of pens labeled "take one," and a few knick-knacks that don't seem to belong anywhere else. The faint smell of coffee and paper hangs in the air. After last night's attempt at sleep, I tell myself I need to get out this morning, do something other than return to cleaning.

"Hey there," says the woman behind the counter, brushing crumbs off her apron. Her silver hair is pulled back in a loose braid, streaks of gray and brown catching the light. Her name tag says *Lody* in alphabet stickers.

"You must be new in town. Got that 'just rolled in' look about you."

I blink. "That obvious, huh?"

"Yeah," she chuckles. "Hazel, right? Beau mentioned someone moving into that flower farm up the ridge. I'm Melody, but you can call me Lody."

"Lody," I repeat with a small smile, tucking the name away.

I drift toward the shelves, not really looking for anything in particular—just soaking in the quiet, bookish charm of the place.

A row of gardening and farm books catch my eye. I pick up a couple: *The Local Flower Gardener* and *Perennials for Small Farms*. Leafing through them, I realize the advice is practical, rooted in real experience rather than glossy social media shots of impossibly perfect blooms. I tuck them under my arm.

From the corner of the shop, I overhear a pair of older ladies chatting softly near the register.

" . . . he's still grumpy as ever," one says, shaking her head. "Beau? Oh, yes. Haven't seen him smile since the '90s."

I pause mid-step, smothering a laugh. Grumpy neighbor Beau is already a local legend, apparently.

On another aisle, a glossy paperback practically jumps out at me from the middle shelf: *Wandering Wild: A Solo Hiker's Guide to the Blue Fern Mountains*. A cartoon bear in a large hat grins from the cover, holding a trail map, and the subtitle read: *For the bold, the curious, and the delightfully unprepared.*

I snort. He'd *love* this. My ex, the complete fool who thought every adventure could be tackled with days of zero preparation. Sold.

I buy it, along with a postcard I don't need, and leave the store with a weird little flutter in my chest. This break was nice, but it's time to go home.

Home. What a weird thought.

Walking back up the gravel drive to the farmhouse, books clutched under my arm, I know what I'll meet.

Inside, I set the books down on the kitchen table, releasing a breath I didn't know I was holding. The floors still carry streaks of the day's cleaning, the counters need another round, and there's the lingering mystery of the mudroom. I'm not sure I'm ready to confront it yet. Not after the mouse.

I roll up my sleeves, tug my hair into a loose bun, and grab a fresh rag and the spray bottle I left by the sink. The farmhouse feels different in the morning light, the shadows stretching longer across the hardwood floors, and I have to stop for a moment to take it in. Each room seems bigger than it did in the morning, quieter, the walls waiting for me to breathe life into them.

"Alright," I whisper to no one but the dust, "one more round. *Maybe.*"

I start with the kitchen, scrubbing the counters until the scent of lemon cleaner mixes with the aroma of old wood. The floor gets a quick sweep and mop. I find another mouse nest in the corner, and after an exaggerated grimace, banish it to the outdoors.

By the time I pause, sweat is beading at my temples. I'm finally starting to get a sense of the rhythm—well, if I ignore all the boxes I probably won't touch for another few weeks. *Baby steps.* This is already an overwhelming venture.

Through the window above the sink, the flower beds stretch toward the horizon, rolling gently into the hills beyond. Everything is painted in honeyed tones. I press my palm to the glass, tracing the mountains with my fingers.

Back in Washington, life had always been louder, yes, but it was beautiful in its own way. The mountains and forests, the endless shades of green, the mist that clung to the valleys like a soft blanket, there was a quiet magic in that complexity. The Pacific Northwest had a way of curing something in you, of layering you with experiences and moments that lingered long after you left. City streets hummed with energy, coffee-scented air, rain-soaked mornings, and friendships that carried you through hard winters. It was layered, nuanced, and alive in a way that shaped me without my noticing.

Here, the world moves differently. The wind, the distant hills, the way the light touches the farmhouse walls—it all demands attention, a slower kind of noticing. I sink onto a chair near the window, letting my shoulders loosen. This quiet . . . is almost disorienting, but in a way that feels good. Every little detail, the way the light shifts across the floor, the distant clatter of a bird hopping through the garden, the soft creak of the farmhouse settling, reminds me that I am somewhere new.

A small smile tugs at my lips.

I shake myself out of the daydream and stand, stretching stiff arms over my head.

The mudroom calls. I know it is a disaster, but ignoring it will not make it any less . . . well, terrifying. Grabbing the broom, a fresh rag, and another bottle of cleaner, I brace myself.

Stepping inside, I squint at the jumble of boots, old garden tools, and what I suspect is an old supply of birdseed.

A spider scuttles across the floor, and I let out a squeak that's equal parts laugh and shriek.

"Yep, this is exactly why they have a mudroom."

I start with the floor, sweeping the dirt and dust into a growing pile. The broom scratches over uneven boards, and my arm aches sooner than I'd like. Next is the shelves, where I find a tangle of ropes, a half-empty bag of nails, and a faded catalog for farm equipment from who-knows-when. I sort, toss, and occasionally grumble commentary to myself. The Marshalls left behind so much . . .

"This is fine," I say to the empty room, though my voice wavers. "Completely manageable. Nothing terrifying. Just a pile of stuff."

By the time I rest against the doorframe to survey my progress, the room looks almost respectable. *Almost*. My shirt has streaks again, dust and cleaner. But even with my hair clinging to my forehead, I feel a tiny surge of triumph. The farmhouse is starting to respond to me, in little ways, room by room. *Thank Jesus there were no more mice.*

I eye the space a moment longer, catching my breath.

By the time I finish surveying the mudroom, my stomach

reminds me that cleaning burns more calories than I expect. I rummage through one of the boxes I'd brought from Washington and find a granola bar, a sad amount of trail mix, and a slightly squished apple. Perfect. Not a feast, but enough to keep me going.

I peel the apple and bite into it, the sweet, crisp flavor grounding me in the moment. With one hand holding my snack and the other pushing the broom, I move on to the pantry. Shelves are lined with dusty jars, some labeled in handwriting I don't recognize. I stack cans, wipe down surfaces, and shuffle through boxes of long-forgotten pasta and rice. The smell of the house mixes with the faint tang of the apple in my mouth, it is strangely comforting.

Halfway through, I am bouncing from one foot to the other, chewing thoughtfully. I look at my watch, just after noon. A few weeks ago, I might have grabbed a quick sandwich on the way between work and yoga class, eating while running from one task to another. I think it is slowly occurring to me just how different things are going to be.

Granola bar in hand, I head to the hallway closet next. Jackets, brooms, and more tools had tumbled into a chaotic pile. I sort, toss, and organize, sneaking bites in between sweeps. By the time the snack is gone, the closet is . . . passable. A small victory, but a victory nonetheless.

A small, leather-bound diary tucked behind a stack of gardening books on the highest shelf catches my eye. Dust rises in a lazy swirl as I drag it free, sneezing as the musty air stirs. The cover is cracked, the corners softened from years of handling, the leather bearing the kind of wear that came only from being loved.

I hold it in my hands longer than I should have, thumb brushing the edge, debating. The Marshalls had left everything it feels—furniture, dishes, memories. Their final letter at closing had been short and gracious: *Don't worry about calling. We want nothing back. By now, we'll be busy with retirement and better horizons.* The words had struck me as final then, but now, standing in their old farmhouse with this diary in my palms, I feel like I am intruding.

Put it back, I tell myself. This isn't mine. And yet...

The weight of it lingers in my grip, heavy with secrets I haven't been invited to know. My thumb finds the strap that keeps it closed, and I play with it, looping and unlooping the leather band, as if the decision lives in the small motion. Guilt prickles sharply. If someone found my journal after I'm gone, would I want a stranger leafing through my words? Probably not.

But the Marshalls aren't just strangers anymore. Clara and Henry Marshall built this place. If I am to build anything here, maybe understanding them matters.

Finally, curiosity tips the scale. I ease the strap free and open to the first page. The ink faded but legible, a neat, looping script. Clara's hand, I guess. The entry dates nearly twenty years ago.

This farm feels like breathing. Henry says we are exactly where we're meant to be.

I draw in a shaky breath. My throat tightens as I think of their final note again—Clara's health, the move to warmer air because of a cancer that stole her breath. Better horizons. The phrase seems almost cruel in hindsight.

I turn another page, guilt still curling in me.

... Henry made it for me today. A small wooden sign for the field at the edge of the meadow. We said that wherever we plant it, love will always bloom there. Even when we're gone.

can't stop smiling. This land . . . it feels like it's ours.

The words leap off the page, alive with hope and promise. I turn the pages slowly, reading fragments of daily life, fleeting moments of joy, the kind of love that makes a house into a home. Piece by piece, I begin to understand why the Marshalls left so suddenly. Not because they didn't love this land, but because life sometimes demanded change before you are ready to say goodbye.

I sit with the diary balancing on my knees, staring at the looping handwriting until the words blur. I can almost picture Henry and Clara, young and in love, shaping this farmhouse the way I am only just beginning to. My chest feels a little tight, which was ridiculous because I never even met them. But now, knowing Henry carved that sign with his own hands, I can't leave it propped in the corner like forgotten décor.

So I heave myself up and retrieve the wooden plank. Somehow, it feels heavier —not just wood, but weighted with all that intention and history. Which, of course, is exactly the kind of thought that makes me roll my eyes. Honestly, the whole thing feels like I've been dropped straight into a cheesy romance novel.

Outside, the sky has gone watercolor—streaks of pink and lavender smudge across the horizon. I plant the sign carefully on the hooks at the edge of the property, fussing with it until it stands straight, sturdy against the wind. I step back, hands on my hips, and try to take it all in—the fields, the hills, the farmhouse glowing warm behind me. Very dramatic. Very main-character energy.

For a beat, I just stand there in the hush, letting the silence wrap around me. My first full day here is done. The work is far from finished, but it settles over me in a good way—like maybe, just maybe, I belong to something that might last.

Back inside, I wipe my hands on the kitchen towel and flick off the lights. On impulse, I peer out the window, where the last streaks of sunset brush over the fields. The sign gleams faintly, solid and sure against the rolling hills.

And then I see him.

Across the way, near the shadow of the tree line, is my neighbor. Broad-shouldered, still as a silhouette cut out of the dusk. A yard tool rests in his hand, glinting faintly. My breath hitches, catching between alarm and . . . curiosity?

For a heartbeat, neither of us move. Then, almost imperceptibly, he tips his head—acknowledgment or dismissal, I can't quite tell—and turns back toward his land.

I exhale, a small thrill zipping through me. Small town, big eyes. Everyone keeping tabs on everyone, even when they pretend not to.

Tomorrow, there'll be more work, weeds, more wondering what I've gotten myself into. But tonight, the farmhouse can breathe easy. The wildflower sign stands steady in the dark, and Beau's quiet presence lingers at the edge of my thoughts like an unfinished sentence.

Hazel

THE BLUE FERN MOUNTAINS WIN

The next morning, a slow-growing brightness works its way through the windows, warmth stretching across my exposed arms and waking me before eight. I blink against it, trying to stretch the last vestiges of sleep from my arms and shoulders, the kind of sleep that feels like it's just a little too short but still enough to make me groggy in the best possible way.

Barefoot, I shuffle into the kitchen, the cool wood pressing against the soles of my feet, sending tiny shivers up my spine. My hand fumbles through a cardboard box that smells faintly of old paper and moving dust, and lands on the jar of instant coffee I've stashed there. Weak, watery, a pale shadow of the rich dark roast I used to nurse in Seattle, but in this moment, it feels like a lifeline. A connection to a past self, a morning ritual I still belong to. I scoop a spoonful into a chipped mug I find in the cupboard, the glaze faded to a robin's-egg blue that doesn't match anything else in the kitchen but feels like it always belonged here, like it has been waiting for me. I pour in the steaming water, letting the aroma curl into the air, a bitter, sweet promise of wakefulness.

The kitchen isn't silent. Beau is somewhere making that

strange clatter of his own. Metal scraping, the occasional hiss, the low thrum of what I assume is an air compressor. I have no real clue. Honestly, I don't care. It is one of the sounds that can make a space feel alive, like the heartbeat of a place. It is familiar now, unfortunately.

I slide into the kitchen chair, the worn wood creaking under me, and lift the guidebook from the table: *Wandering Wild: A Solo Hiker's Guide to the Blue Fern Mountains*. The glossy pages smell faintly of ink and adventure, a scent that makes me feel like anything was possible. I thumb through until I find the section I've dog-eared:

Trail #3—Fern Creek Lookout. Moderate Difficulty. Sweeping Views. Magical Vibes.

My fingers hover over the words, tracing the lines as if I can memorize the magic just by touching it.

Magical vibes. Exactly what I need. After yesterday's chaos —bleach stains on my sleeves, a mouse skittering across the countertop, and the neighbor's glare that says, loud and clear, *I'd rather wrestle barbed wire than talk to you*—I need a reminder that the world still holds a bit of wonder. Something untouched. Something that doesn't care if I spill cleaning solution on my shoes or cry over a half-empty moving box.

My eyes drift to the window again, to the mountains in the distance. I can almost hear the wind in the pines, a soft susurration that promises secrets if I am willing to listen.

I tap the book nervously against the table. Unpacking can wait. Laundry can wait. Emails, deadlines, to-do lists—all of it can wait. Today is about this, about finding something new, about taking a breath so deep it makes my chest ache in the best way. Today is about wandering.

I drain the last sip of bitter coffee, letting the warmth slide down my throat and spread through me like liquid courage. I tuck the guidebook under my arm, grab the small daypack I'd prepared last night with snacks and a water bottle, and pause for a moment to let the gravity of it all hit me. I am here. I have made it. And the mountains, sprawling and quiet, seem to nod their approval.

A smile creeps across my face. Today, I am going to the trail. Today, I am going to see what these mountains have to offer.

"How hard can it be?" I murmur to no one, tugging my sneakers tight like I'm gearing up for battle. I even give them a solemn nod, as if these shoes have promised to carry me up mountains and down valleys and maybe even into sainthood.

The first ten minutes feel like magic. Crisp air, clean and pine-scented, fills my lungs and makes me feel alive in a way that no cup of coffee ever could. The trail is dotted with cheerful wooden signs, their paint peeling a little, cartoon bears grinning from the corners as if they know some secret about life I haven't learned yet. I hum, snap a photo of moss clinging stubbornly to a tree root, and pause dramatically to write a mental journal entry about how grounded I feel.

Then comes the incline.

And it doesn't stop.

I grab a tree trunk for leverage, heaving breaths so loud I'm sure the squirrels are writing complaints about me in their little squirrel journals. Flipping through my guidebook for something, anything, to encourage myself, I find the cartoon bear again giving a tiny thumbs-up. I glare at him. Really? Him? This smug little thing with his cheerful face and perfect posture?

By the thirty-minute mark, I am practically a contortionist crawling on hands and knees over a slope that clearly has a vendetta against moderate hikers. My water bottle makes a daring escape from my backpack, rolling downhill like it's fleeing from responsibility. I salute it silently, thinking maybe it will find a better, more hydrated life somewhere down there.

"This was a mistake," I wheeze, collapsing dramatically onto a bed of ferns, arms splayed, heaving like I just ran a marathon through a hedge maze. I lie there for a long, heroic moment, imagining myself as a tragic cartoon character whose sole purpose is to provide comic relief. A chipmunk darts past, tail flicking with what I swear is disdain, and I imagine it sending smoke signals to the forest council about my reckless life choices.

Thighs burning, lungs screaming, and pride swelling like an overinflated balloon animal, a weird grin spreads across my face. I climbed a *thing*. I left the house. My sneakers are probably going to be tragic works of modern art after this. But I'm here. And I am not quitting.

Eventually, I haul myself upright, mud streaks across my arms, sweat plastering my hair to my forehead, and stagger toward the next incline. Each step is a negotiation, each breath a treaty, until I reach a small rise. I throw my arms into the air and yell at the trees, "I am a silly goose—but I am a stubborn silly goose!"

A crow caws somewhere, and I pretend it's cheering me on, like a feathery, judgmental personal trainer. A small gust of wind ruffles my hair and fills me with the kind of victory you only get when you climb something steep, painful, and absolutely unnecessary.

I continue, wobbling like a newborn deer over jagged roots and rocks, feeling the burn in my calves like tiny, sadistic firebrands. I step on a loose stone, almost face-plant into a mud puddle, and imagine the squirrels telling tales of the day a human failed spectacularly on Fern Creek Lookout. And yet —I keep going. Because there's some stubborn spark in me that refuses to give in to gravity, exhaustion, or common sense.

Hours—or maybe fifteen minutes, who's counting—later, I make it to what the guidebook calls the "lookout." Except the lookout is mostly a patch of rocks with a few trees obstructing the view, and the magical sweep of Fern Creek is more like "ferns vaguely in the distance." I sit down on a rock, triumphant yet humiliated, and the bear on the back cover seems to wink at me, a speech bubble reading, *"You did it! Even if you didn't go far, you went."*

"Shut up, bear!" I grin, resting my back against a tree, my backpack half-draped over my shoulders, my water bottle squished under me like a defeated companion—or it would be, if it hadn't run away from our success here. I take in the forest, the ridiculous cartoonish signage, the chipmunks, the stubborn moss, and the sun bouncing off the leaves, and I feel it all—the ache, the sweat, the triumph, the absurdity.

Sliding back into the truck, sunburned, sore, needles poking every exposed patch of skin, I peel off my socks like I'm defusing explosives, grimacing at each burnished fiber of fabric.

The air-conditioning is a luxury I never knew I missed, and I sit back, laughing nervously and silently praying that tomorrow my muscles remember how to move without protest.

Somewhere deep in my bag, my guidebook lies speckled with dirt and debris, the cartoon bear still grinning like an idiot, and I think to myself, maybe the view isn't perfect. Maybe I didn't conquer a summit. But today? Today, I showed up. And that, my friends, is a victory worth every muddy step, every slipping water bottle, and every judgy squirrel glare.

Beau

DINER, ACCIDENTS, AND YOU

The local diner is buzzing with the sounds of sizzling bacon and clinking silverware. The smell wafts through the air, warm and inviting, wrapping around me like a favorite old flannel. I sit at my usual booth in the back, the vinyl seat sticky from years of grease and coffee spills, but it feels like home. I nurse a cup of black coffee and shove a forkful of scrambled eggs into my mouth, savoring the way they're perfectly fluffy.

My mind drifts to the new neighbor—Hazel. She's been in town for all of a week, and already, I can tell she's going to be a problem. When I first saw her pull up, a beat-up truck stuffed with bags and boxes, I figured she'd be like all the others who think running a flower farm is some kind of romantic getaway.

But the way she stood there, staring at that rundown farmhouse with wide eyes, told me she didn't have a clue what she was getting into.

"She'll be out of here by the end of the season," I grumble to myself, stabbing at my plate with a little more force than necessary.

The waitress, Saffron, raises an eyebrow at me from

behind the counter. "You talking about that sweet girl who bought Pine & Petal?"

"Sweet? She's naive."

Saffron rolls her eyes, pouring herself a cup of coffee. "She's got spunk, Beau. Give her a chance."

I shake my head, I know I'm stubborn as a mule. "You don't know what it takes to run a farm, Saffron. It's hard work. Backbreaking work. That place—Pine & Petal—is a disaster. I have seen *three* people come in, and leave the same week. They don't even unpack."

She smirks. "If you ask me, she's better than most. Not every day does someone dive into farming with zero experience. That's brave."

"Brave or stupid," I grunt, squeezing the mug until my knuckles whiten.

She chuckles, dropping a stack of napkins with a soft thump. "Like how she went hiking in the Blue Fern Mountains alone, armed with nothing but a water bottle of lemonade and a single granola bar?"

I exhale, a long, bitter sound. Of course she knows. Everybody knows. In a town this small, you sneeze funny and your cousin's dog walker will have a full report before lunch.

"I know," I state. "She made it halfway before she turned back, never even found the damn lookout."

Saffron grins. "Hey, she did make it somewhere—even if it was just the rest area. It can be hard to tell on those trails."

"Barely."

"Still counts."

"You don't go wandering up those trails alone unless you know what you're doing. Even locals get turned around sometimes. She could've gotten hurt."

"So you *have* been paying attention," Saffron hums, not unkindly.

I shoot her a look, but she's already moving on, reorganizing a stack of food catalogs like she didn't just try to unearth some deeper truth from my concern. But it's not like that.

"She just . . . she doesn't know what she's gotten herself into," I say finally, quieter now. "These mountains ain't a fairytale. It's early mornings, late nights, and everything in between breaking down when you least expect it."

I force myself to take a sip, but the coffee burns my tongue, reminding me of the flare that's creeping in, that familiar ache in my joints. I feel it in my hands first, a dull throb that builds into something sharper. I flex my fingers under the table, hoping to ease the stiffness before anyone notices.

"Still grumbling about the flowers?" A voice cuts through my thoughts, and I look up to see Steve, the town's mechanic, sliding into the seat across from me.

"Just saying the new neighbor is going to have a hard time of it," I reply, trying to sound nonchalant.

"Or maybe she'll surprise you," Steve retorts, a smirk playing on his lips. "I wouldn't underestimate a woman determined to make her mark."

"Women come and go in this town," I scoff. "They don't stick around once they realize the work involved."

Steve chuckles, and I can't help but feel a little defensive. "You just wait. I'll bet you a month's worth of breakfast that she won't make it through the first winter."

"Deal," he says, shaking my hand. "But I'll be surprised if you're right."

We chat a bit more, but my mind wanders back to Hazel. I can picture her now, all wide-eyed and hopeful, but that won't last long. She'll realize that the idyllic life of farming is anything but, especially when the weather turns and the work piles up.

After finishing my breakfast and downing another cup of coffee, I reluctantly pay the bill and head back outside. The air is brisk, and I pull my jacket tighter around me as I make my way back to the orchard.

The diner's not far from Daffon Street, maybe a fifteen-minute walk if you take it slow—and I usually do. Not 'cause I like to dawdle, but because this town's got a way of pulling memories out of you when you least expect it.

I pass Gideon's Hardware, where the front windows are stacked with seed catalogs and hand-painted signs about propane tanks. Used to come here every Saturday with my Pa when I was a kid. He'd park me on the stool by the counter with a cream soda while he talked shop with old man Gideon. That stool's still there, by the way. Squeaks when you turn too fast. There is a new hardware shop—I bet Hazel will poke around—but we true towners, we pick the ole' Gideon.

Across the street, *Blythe's Barber & Billiards* still has that half-lit neon sign in the window—just the "B" and "illiards" glowing. Half the fellas in town have their names sharpied on the wall above the pool table from tournaments past. I haven't set foot in there in years.

I take the shortcut through the churchyard behind *Mount Fern Chapel*. The bell tower's quiet now, but I swear I can still hear it if the wind's right. Used to ring every Sunday morning when my mama would drag me, clean shirt and all, to sit in the same pew our family had for three generations. There's lichen growing on the gravestones now, old names partially worn away. This place doesn't rush. It holds time.

Once I'm past the chapel, it's just a gravel road that winds toward the ridge—meandering past wildflower fields and weathered fence posts and the occasional nosy goat.

The orchard comes into view just beyond the rise. From here, the house looks quiet, slouched under the weight of years but still standing. I spot the trees first, their limbs bare and dark against the overcast sky, rows and rows of them reaching like tired arms. There's work waiting for me. There's always work.

I catch a glimpse of Hazel, her back to me, bent over the earth like she's searching for buried treasure.

A sharp breath catches in my throat as I eye her working, the determination in her posture undeniable. But then she straightens, her shovel flashing faintly in the early morning brightness, and her expression changes as she digs deeper into the soil.

"Hey! Be careful!" I call out, but my voice doesn't carry far enough.

Before I can take a step toward her, I see it happen—she digs down hard, and the ground shifts. Suddenly, a loud *crack* echoes through the air, and water starts gushing up from the ground like a geyser.

"Shit!" I curse, the reality of the situation hitting me like a punch to the gut.

I hurry to her, the pain in my hands forgotten as adrenaline kicks in. "What did you do?" I shout, frustration bubbling up.

Hazel turns, wide-eyed, and for a moment, we're locked in a gaze that says so much more than words. Her shock morphs into realization, and she drops the shovel, sprinting toward the rushing water, her face flushes with panic.

"I didn't mean to!" she stammers, her voice rising above the roar of the water. "I thought I was just—"

"Thought you were just what?" I snap, trying to keep my composure, but the anger builds. "Digging up a century-old irrigation system that connects our properties? Because that's exactly what you did!"

She looks genuinely distraught, and for a moment, I see a glimpse of the vulnerability I noticed before. But then I shake my head, pushing past sympathy, knowing this is going to be a major issue.

I shout over the water, cutting through the chaos. "We need to contain this before it floods your farm and mine!"

As Hazel scrambles to find something to help, I grit my

teeth as the pain in my joints intensifies. I'm not about to let a rookie flower farmer ruin everything I've worked for.

Hazel is tripping over herself as she rushes to grab buckets. I can see the panic in her every move, the way she fumbles with the handle of an old tin pail before running back toward the water, looking entirely unsure of what the hell she's supposed to do.

Water is spreading fast, soaking into the already-soft earth, and if we don't stop it soon, both of our properties are going to be in deep trouble. I press my fingers to my temple, biting back a curse as my joints throb like fire. The pain is intensifying, crawling up my wrists like a relentless vise.

"Buckets aren't gonna cut it," I grit out, stepping into the mess. The cold water seeps into my boots, but I don't care. "We need to shut off the main valve."

"Where is it?" Hazel's eyes go wide.

"On *your* property."

"Oh." She blinks.

"Oh," I mimic, because *damn it, woman*, now is not the time for realizations. "Come on!"

I don't wait for her to follow. I'm already moving, slogging through the mud toward where I *hope* the old shutoff valve is still buried. Hazel rushes after me, her breathing uneven.

"How was I supposed to know that pipe was there?" she protests. "It's not like the Marshalls left me a guidebook on where everything is buried."

I whip around so fast she nearly crashes into me. "It's called common sense, Hazel. You don't go hacking into the ground without checking what's under it first."

Her lips press into a thin line, and for a second, I think she's going to snap back, but then her shoulders drop slightly. "But how can I check if I don't . . . dig?" she says, glancing at the flood.

I stare at her for a beat longer than necessary. I don't have time to decipher whatever emotion is flashing across her face, so I turn back around and keep moving.

We reach the spot where I *think* the old shutoff valve is buried. The last time I saw it was years ago, back when my Pa was still alive. He and the Marshalls used this irrigation system for decades before switching to their own wells.

Hazel hovers beside me as I kneel down and start digging, ignoring the sharp protest of my body. The soil is soaked, making it easier to move, but the deeper I go, the worse the pain gets. My knees tremble, the inflammation making every movement feel like I'm working with stiff, rusted gears.

I suck in a breath and keep going.

"Here." Hazel suddenly drops to her knees next to me, grabbing a second shovel. "Let me help."

I nearly tell her no, that I've got it, but the words get caught in my throat. I *don't* have it. And if I don't let her help, I'll be here all damn day. So, instead of arguing, I nod sharply, and together, we dig. The silence between us is thick, stretched tight like a wire ready to snap. But then, after what feels like forever, I hit something hard with the tip of the shovel.

"Got it," I grunt. Hazel leans in, wiping mud from her cheek, and together, we clear away enough dirt to reveal the old metal valve.

"Okay," I exhale, wiping sweat from my brow. "Now, we turn it."

I grip the valve, feeling the stubborn metal bite into my palms. Hazel braces her shoulder against mine. Together we push and twist. The handle resists, groaning under our effort.

A shudder runs through the pipes. Water sputters, hisses, and then—silence. The flow cuts off completely.

Hazel wipes her hands on her jeans, her face streaked with dirt. "Well," she says, breathless, "that was a disaster."

I huff out something that might be a laugh—low, rough, unexpected. "Yeah."

Something passes between us. A quiet understanding. A truce?

"I'll fix it," she says, nodding toward the mess she made. "I'll figure out how to reroute things."

I study her for a second. The woman has no clue what she's doing, and yet, she doesn't back down.

I shake my head, pushing to my feet despite the sharp protest in my knees.

"No," I say, sighing. "You won't."

"I—" Her face falls.

"I will."

She blinks up at me. "What?"

I roll my shoulders, already regretting what I'm about to say. "I'll help you fix it. If you try to do this on your own, you'll end up making it worse."

"Okay," she murmurs.

I don't know why I said it. I saw something in her today that I didn't expect.

Either way, I know one thing for sure. Hazel might not have a clue what she's doing, but she's not going anywhere. And like it or not . . . I might just have to get used to having a neighbor. And to be honest, that enrages me.

The heat is already rising, chasing off the last of the cool morning air as I trudge back toward my farm. My boots are damp with dew, my patience is thinning fast, and the day has only just begun.

Hazel's mess will take time to fix—time I don't have. I roll my shoulders, trying to shake off the tension. The orchard won't wait. If I linger here stewing over what can't be changed, I'll only fall behind.

By the time I reach the rows of apple trees, the haze has

lifted, and sunlight spills across the branches. The air is sweet, tinged with the sharpness of fertilizer. Late summer is a test of endurance, harvest close enough to taste, yet still demanding every ounce of work. I trail my fingers over the firm curve of a low-hanging apple as I pass, checking for blemishes. If all goes well, the season will hold.

I reach for the barn door and tug it open, the scent of fertilizer and hay greeting me like an old friend. The equipment is lined up where it always is, organized in a way that only I understand. I grab the sprayer for the orchard and haul it toward the field, the weight of it pulling at my already tortured muscles.

I spend the next hour working through the orchard, spraying for pests, checking the soil, and making mental notes of which trees need extra care. I try to focus, but Hazel's voice keeps creeping into my thoughts, her stubborn determination, the way she dug beside me without hesitation, the flicker of understanding in her eyes when she saw my hands shake.

I shove the thought aside. She's not my problem. Her farm isn't my problem.

Except, now it is.

I wipe the sweat from my forehead and step back from the last row of trees. Then I start over, this time with a bucket of whitewash in one hand and an old brush in the other. Some say it's outdated, but it's the way my Pa did it, and his before him. You coat the bark—especially on the young trees—to protect them. Simple as that.

I kneel beside a sapling at the edge of the orchard, dip the brush, and drag the chalky paint up the trunk. The smell of lime hangs sharp in the air.

"Sunscald," I think aloud. That's what it's for. The wood splits. Weakens the tree. From a distance, it looks like nothing —just pale or cracked bark—but it leaves the tree open to rot, insects, and a slow death.

The next tree is one of the older ones—gnarled, tilting slightly. I rest my hand against its rough bark, then get back to work.

Tree after tree, I move down the row, the rhythm steady. Dip. Brush. Dip. Brush. It's the kind of task that usually lets my thoughts drift, but today they circle the same place.

I scrub harder at a knot in the bark, jaw tight. *She's not my problem.*

And yet . . . here I am, staring down trees.

Just as I'm about to head toward the barn, I hear the sound of tires trying to make it up my less-than-friendly driveway.

I see a familiar old pickup truck rolling up. Clyde Wilson.

He sticks his head out of the window before the truck even comes to a stop, his weathered face already set in a grimace. "Beau, I hate to bother ya, but I got a problem."

I resist the urge to groan. "What kind of problem?"

Clyde swings the truck door open and steps out, dust coating his overalls. "Damn tractor's acting up again. Can't get the tiller to engage properly, and I need it running by tomorrow if I'm gonna stay on schedule."

I run a hand down my face. I *really* don't have time for this today. But Clyde's been a friend of my family for years, and around here, neighbors help neighbors—even when they've got too much on their own plate. I realize how that contradicts my thoughts before I look up at him.

"Alright." I release a breath, already sensing the day stretching longer. "Let's take a look."

Clyde grins, slapping my shoulder. "Knew I could count on ya, boy."

My hands—already stiff, already tired. This thing's gonna take more than just a wrench and my grit.

With a groan, I dig into my back pocket and pull out my phone. There's only one person I trust with this kind of job who won't ask a million questions or treat me like I'm fragile. I thumb through my contacts and tap the name: *Jonas*.

It rings twice before a deep voice picks up, low and scratchy like gravel under tires. "Well, if it ain't cousin Beau. You finally decide to admit I'm better lookin', or you need somethin'?"

A laugh sneaks out. "Tractor's throwing a fit. Clyde's got it parked halfway out his barn lookin' like it's tryin' to escape. Think you can swing by?"

Jonas doesn't miss a beat. "That the old Massey Ferguson he won't let die?"

"The one and only."

"I'm twenty minutes out. Bringin' the good tools. You got coffee?"

"I'll make a fresh pot."

There's a pause, then his voice softens just a notch. "How's the hands today?"

The slight tremor in my thumb pulses, the stiffness curled into my knuckles. "They're fine," I lie, because that's easier than the truth.

Another beat. Jonas doesn't push, just lets the silence stretch.

"I'll be there soon," he says.

We don't talk much about our condition. Jonas has carried it since his twenties—he knows the road I'm walking better than most. Doesn't need to ask. He just gets it.

Some folks dress it up with medical terms, but to me it's simple: joints wearing out like fence posts rotting at the base. You don't always see the damage right off, but it's there, slow and steady, until one day the whole thing gives.

I hang up and pocket the phone, staring at the mountains in the distance for a long moment.

Clyde comes back around the corner, arms full of mismatched tools and zero coordination.

"You call in backup?" he asks.

I shake my head, following him toward his truck. The hell Hazel caused is already looming over my day, but first, I've got an old farmer to help and a tractor to fix.

And with the way things are going, I doubt this will be the last interruption . . .

Hazel

CITY DIET

I prop my phone between my shoulder and ear as I pace the kitchen.

"Hazel, honey, you can't seriously think this is sustainable." My mom's voice filters through the speaker, her tone caught between worry and exasperation. "You don't know anything about farming. You could come back to Seattle, find something else. Something *stable*."

I roll my eyes and flop down into one of the kitchen chairs. "Mom. We've been over this. I *don't* want to come back."

"But—"

"Nope," I cut her off before she can start listing all the reasons why leaving my corporate job was reckless. "I'm figuring it out. It's just . . . a learning curve." A steep, nearly-vertical learning curve that may or may not result in me killing half the flowers.

She sighs, the kind only a mother can perfect—long, dramatic, dripping with I just want what's best for you. "And how's that going so far?"

I hesitate, chewing on my bottom lip. I can lie. Tell her

everything is going smoothly. But she'll see right through it, and honestly, I kind of *need* to vent.

"Well . . . I may have accidentally dug up an old irrigation system that connects to my neighbor's farm, nearly flooded both our properties, and now he has to help me fix it. I may also be completely ignoring the flowers and all the outside work because . . . I have no idea what I am doing—yet."

There's a long pause. Then—"Oh, honey."

"I *know*." I rub my temples. "It was an accident, and I *am* going to learn how to do this properly. I just—"

"You don't have to prove anything to anyone," Mom interjects, her voice softening. "Especially not to me. You know we'd love to have you back. Your old boss even asked about you the other day. There may be an opening to that dream job and—" She stops, as if forcing herself to think about her next words. "Oh, Hazel . . . they'd take you back in a heartbeat."

A pang of guilt twists in my chest, but I push it down. "That's not the point."

"Then what is? Liam?"

I close my eyes. "This is my long run, Mom. I'm not coming back. I *want* to be here."

She goes quiet for a moment, then shifts tactics so quickly I nearly get whiplash. "So, tell me about this neighbor of yours."

I groan. "Mom."

"What? I'm just making conversation."

I snort. "No, you're fishing for gossip."

"I would never," she gasps dramatically.

Which is the furthest from the truth. My mom is a gossip hoarder, and she loves every minute of tea time.

"Uh-huh."

"Alright, fine." She chuckles. "But really, who is he?"

I tilt back in my chair, letting my head fall against the worn wooden slats. "Beau Rosewood. Owns the orchard next door. Kind of grumpy. Very rugged. Not exactly thrilled that I exist."

"Well, that's rude."

I huff a laugh. "I think I'm more of a nuisance than anything."

"But is he *good-looking*?" Mom hums, clearly enjoying this.

"Mom."

"What? I'm just asking!"

"Yes, he's good-looking." I rub my temples. "But he's also gruff and broody and acts like I showed up just to ruin his life."

"A *single* man?" she whispers. I can practically hear the excitement brewing.

"A *grumpy* single man," I correct.

I only know this because the Marshalls' note didn't skimp on the details . . . *including him.*

"Sounds like a man who needs a good home-cooked meal and a little kindness."

"Sounds like a man who wants to be *left alone.*"

"Oh, honey," she tsks. "You're in a small town now. Nobody gets left alone."

I roll my eyes, but I know she's right.

"Did you know his family has owned that orchard for generations? Everyone in town adores him." I suppress a giggle. "That's hard to believe."

"Well, I am sure he's got a heart of gold underneath all that gruffness. And . . ." She pauses for effect. "He's single."

I groan again. "Mom—"

"Fine, fine. So, tell me—how's the farm? Really?"

I straighten my spine and say, "It's good. Hard work, but good."

Mom doesn't believe me. I can tell by the way she exhales through her nose. But she doesn't push. Not this time. Instead, she circles back to the topic she *really* wants to discuss.

"I'm just curious. You said he's grumpy, but he did help you today, didn't he?"

I hesitate, remembering the way he showed up, the way he stepped in when I had no clue what to do. And how, even though he acted like he didn't want to, he let me help when he needed it.

"He did," I admit. "But . . ."

"But what?"

I hesitate again, chewing on my lip. I don't know why I even noticed, but something about the way Beau worked—about the way he *didn't* work—stood out. The way he avoided certain movements, like he knew they'd hurt.

"Hazel?" Mom prompts.

"Nothing. It's nothing." I shake myself.

"I just don't want you to struggle."

My eyes land on the empty fridge. *Literally empty.*

A slow realization creeps up my spine. I *haven't* gone grocery shopping. I got so caught up in the disaster with the water that I completely forgot about feeding myself.

I open a cabinet, hoping for a miracle. All the food I brought with me has been eaten up.

Well, shit . . .

"Mom, I gotta go."

"Go? Where? It's getting late."

"I, uh . . . forgot to buy food."

Silence. Then, a gasp of horror. "Hazel Lorelai—it's been a week! What in the hell have you been nourishing yourself with? Dust and granola bars?"

"I know! I got distracted! I had food with me. I just, I haven't shopped yet."

Mom makes a disapproving noise. "You see? This is exactly why you need to come back to Seattle. I bet you haven't even eaten all day."

"Mom, I have to go if I'm gonna fix that." I rub my temples again.

"Fine," she murmurs. "But promise me you'll get real food, not just coffee and whatever sad pastry they sell at that tiny town café."

I grin, grabbing my keys. I want to tell her it's a diner and not a café, but I ignore my need to be right. "No promises."

"I love you, honey. Call me tomorrow?"

"I will," I say, stepping out onto the porch. "Love you, too."

I hang up, exhaling. *The town diner it is.*

Fifteen minutes later, I push open the heavy glass door of Love & Biscuits Diner, and the scent of coffee and fried food immediately wraps around me.

The place is buzzing—locals chatting, forks scraping against plates, the low hum of country music playing in the background.

A few heads turn as I step inside. I feel the weight of small-town curiosity settle on me, and I force myself to smile as I make my way to the counter. But one person stood out . . . *Beau.*

Sitting in a corner booth, arms crossed, a plate of half-eaten food in front of him. He looks just as gruff and broody as he did earlier, but now, in the warm light of the diner, I notice the exhaustion beneath it. He squeezes a ton of honey into what I can only assume is hot tea. *Interesting.* So he is a *fancy* grumpy man.

He hasn't seen me yet. For a brief moment, I consider turning around. Maybe slipping back out the door before he realizes I'm here. Too late. His gaze lifts, locking onto mine. His expression doesn't change—not at first. But there's a flicker of recognition, a quick assessment, and then, like clockwork, that slight furrow of disapproval.

I square my shoulders and lift my chin. I'm not letting Mr. Grumpy Tea Boy ruin my first real meal of the day.

So, I walk up to the counter, order a grilled cheese and fries—extra crispy, my favorite diner meal even in my mid-thirties, and very *pointedly* do not look at him. But I can *feel* his eyes on me. And for some ridiculous reason, my heart kicks up a little faster.

The woman behind the counter has a pink-and-white name tag, slightly worn. It displays her name in bold letters—*Maggie*. Below it reads: *Owner*.

She hands me a brown paper bag with a warm smile. "Here you go, sweetheart. Grilled cheese and fries, extra crispy, just like you asked. Can I interest you in some tea to go? We have a new shipment all the way from Havenwood—I hear the Sterling is a good combo with plenty of sugar. I can even add ice!"

"Thank you, but I am okay," I say, returning the smile as I slide a few bills across the counter.

"You settling in alright?" she asks, wiping her hands on her apron.

I hesitate for a second, but before I can answer, someone else cuts in from a nearby table.

"Oh, she's the one who messed up the water lines on Beau's property, right?"

Heat rushes to my cheeks as a couple of old men chuckle over their coffee. Fantastic. My mistake is already town gossip.

Maggie shoots them a look. "Oh, hush, Hank. Like *you've* never dug up the wrong thing on your farm."

The old man—Hank, apparently—just grins. "Sure, but I've been here long enough to know better."

I grip my paper bag a little tighter, biting back the urge to argue. Instead, I plaster on a polite smile. "Well, I *am* new. So, guess I'll have to learn the hard way."

Hank chuckles. "That's the spirit."

I offer a quick thanks to Maggie and turn for the door, eager to escape before I make more of a fool of myself. I'm *almost* free, my fingers just brushing the handle, and then my foot catches on something. The damn *entry mat*. The next thing

I know, I'm stumbling forward, my knees buckling as my ankle twists. The paper bag flies out of my hands. I make a noise somewhere between a squeak and a curse as I brace for impact. But before I can hit the floor, strong hands grab my arms. A rough, intentional grip steadies me, keeping me upright. My breath catches. I don't have to look up to know who it is.

His hands are warm, solid. His grip firm but careful, like he knows exactly how much strength to use. For a second, neither of us move. *He really is out of some damn rugged romance novel.*

Then he clears his throat. "You alright?"

I finally force myself to look up, and regret it instantly. Beau Rosewood is *way* too close.

His eyes, sharp and unreadable, flick over me, like he's checking for damage. I swear I see something linger there—concern, maybe? But it's gone before I can make sense of it.

"I—I'm fine," I stammer, stepping back, suddenly hyper-aware of how warm my face feels. "Just . . . graceful as always."

His lips press into something that's *almost* a smirk.

"Damn mat's been a tripping hazard for years. I keep telling myself I'll replace it." Maggie moans from behind the counter.

"That's the most excitement this diner's seen in weeks," Hank cackles.

"Glad I could entertain." I swipe my food bag from where it landed on the floor

Beau shifts, rubbing the back of his neck. "You should be more careful."

"Wow. *Thanks* for the insight." I narrow my eyes.

"Just saying." One of his brows lift, amused by my attitude. "This town's too small for you to be falling all over it."

"Noted." I tighten my grip on my bag before spinning on my heel and pushing out the door, my face still burning.

The last thing I hear before the door swings shut is Maggie's voice.

"Beau, you're supposed to *flirt* with the girl, not scold her."

I don't dare look back.

By the time I get home, the embarrassment has mostly worn off. *Mostly.* I stomp up the farmhouse steps, muttering under my breath as I unlock the door.

"Be careful," I mock, tossing my keys onto the counter. "Like I *planned* on tripping over the world's deadliest doormat."

Shaking my head, I grab a glass from the cabinet, filling it from the tap and head out to the back porch, my paper bag of slightly squished food tucked under my arm.

The night air is cool, carrying the faint scent of wildflowers. Fireflies flicker in the distance, tiny golden sparks in the darkness. I settle onto the creaky wooden steps, setting my food beside me. For a moment, I just sit there, breathing it all in.

I reach for my fries, shoving one into my mouth. Salty, crispy, still warm. *Perfect.*

But after a few bites, my throat feels dry. I hesitate, staring at the glass of well water beside me. I am out of the bottled water I brought with me from Washington.

My city-raised instincts immediately screamed *do not trust it!*

But I haven't had the time to buy bottled water. And I forgot to grab something to drink at the diner. I'm regretting denying that tea. And now I am sitting here, parched and debating whether this is how I die—tragically poisoned by *farm water.*

On the neighboring property, I can just make out the silhouette of Beau's barn under the moonlight. He drinks this stuff. *He's still alive.* That logic feels shaky, but I'm desperate.

With a deep breath, I squeeze my eyes shut and take a cautious sip. And then another. And then, because I'm *so* thirsty, I just go for it, drinking half the glass in one go. I lower it, waiting. This tastes like . . . iron? *Does that even make sense?*

Five seconds pass. No immediate death. No sudden poisoning. *Huh.* I set the glass down, feeling oddly victorious, and turn back to my dinner.

Maybe I *can* do this. Maybe I *can* make this place work. And yet, as I glance at the barn, I can't shake the feeling that my biggest challenge in Maple Hollow won't be running this farm. It'll be dealing with Beau Rosewood.

The smug sense of victory lasts approximately *three minutes*. Then my gut makes a noise. A deep, foreboding gurgle. I freeze, mid-bite of grilled cheese. *Oh no. Another gurgle. A sharp twist. And then—disaster.*

Panic surges through me as I lurch to my feet, nearly knocking over the glass of traitorous well water. My body enters full-on Mayday mode, and every internal alarm is blaring the same urgent message: bathroom. Immediately.

"Shit, shit, shit—"

I abandon my food entirely and take off, sprinting into the house. The old wooden floor groans beneath my frantic footsteps as I fumble down the hall, yanking the door to the bathroom where I am humbled in the most violent, undignified way possible. I *knew* I shouldn't have trusted the well water. I *knew* it.

Beau Rosewood might have an iron stomach, but clearly, mine is still on a city diet. *Oh God.* What if this happens *every time* I drink it?

I can't *live* like this. I need bottled water.

A *filter*. A priest, maybe, to cleanse the well of whatever vengeful spirits are trying to kill me.

Welcome to farm life, Hazel. This is going great.

Beau

STUBBORN AS A ROSEWOOD

I knew fixing the irrigation system was going to be a pain in the ass. I just didn't expect it to nearly break *me* in the process. I stretch my hands slowly, testing the damage.

The stiffness settled in last night, creeping in like it always does when I push too hard. Now, my fingers feel thick, swollen, like my own skin is working against me. My joints ache deep, a raw, grinding sort of pain, and my knees aren't much better. I might as well be turning into a freaking apple tree. I almost laugh at the idea.

Stupid. I *know* better.

But I couldn't just leave the system in shambles. Hazel might not have a clue what she's doing, but I do. And my land —*our* land—needs water outside of our own well systems.

I spend the whole day fixing what she tore up, crouching and digging and hauling pipes around like I didn't have a body that liked to punish me for *existing*.

And now? I'm paying for it. I exhale slowly, pressing my hands against the counter, trying to ground myself through the wave of pain. The coolness of the counter seeps into my skin. It feels like the only thing motivating me to hang on.

The supply run into town isn't happening today. No

chance I'm making it up and down the feedstore stairs like this. I send a quick text to my buddy—*Can't make it today. Busy*—then toss my phone onto the table and lower myself into a chair with a barely-contained grimace.

A knock at the door makes me stiffen.

Then, without waiting for a response, the door creaks open.

"Beau?"

Hazel.

Of course, it's Hazel.

I turn my head just enough to see her standing there, a to-go tray in one hand, a curious look on her face. *I hate small-town closeness.*

"Didn't exactly invite you in."

She steps inside anyway, kicking the door shut behind her. "Yeah, well, I figured you'd find a reason not to answer if I knocked again."

"Ever hear of respecting boundaries?" I scowl.

"Ever hear of being neighborly? Besides, I have been in and out of here all day while we fixed the irrigation system." She strides over and sets the tray on the table in front of me. The smell of coffee drifts up, rich and warm. "Brought you something."

"Why?" I eye it suspiciously, ignoring her *"we"* knowing well it was *me*.

She shrugs, pulling out a chair across from me. "Because you helped me fix my screw-up."

My muscles tighten. I reach for the coffee, mostly to give my hands something to do. The cup is warm, the heat bleeding.

People always want something from me.

A favor, a discount during apple season, a little extra effort on my behalf because they think I should be grateful they are including me at all. I learned young that most folks don't see me as an equal—they either pity me, thinking I need their help, or they see an easy target. More than once, I have been talked into a raw deal under the guise of kindness. *"We'd ask someone else, but we know you'd do it right."*

And when I finally started saying no? When I stopped letting people take advantage of me or look at my condition as a charity case opportunity, they decided I was bitter. Unfriendly. Short-tempered.

So maybe I am. Maybe I am just a pained grump.

Hazel studies me, her head tilting. "You don't look so good, Beau."

"I always look like this."

"That's . . . not reassuring."

I take a slow sip of coffee, ignoring her scrutiny. She's *too* observant, and I don't like it.

After a beat of silence, she moves forward, resting her elbows on the table.

"You know, for someone who clearly needs help, you sure do go out of your way to avoid it."

"I don't need help!" I set my cup down harder than necessary.

"Right. That's why you're sitting here looking like you lost a fight with a tractor."

"Or spent all morning fixing a problem I didn't cause." I glare.

She meets it head-on, completely unfazed.

This woman. She's got no business prying, no reason to care about what I'm dealing with. But she *does*—I can see it in the way she's studying me, trying to piece together the truth I refuse to say out loud. And worse? Some confused, exhausted part of me almost wants to let her.

Hazel doesn't look away. She locks in, stubborn as a damn weed that won't quit growing, waiting me out.

I run a hand over my face, gripping the coffee cup. My body protests, stiff and slow as I lift it again, but I don't let it show. *Mostly.*

Her eyes flicker down. I can *feel* the gears turning in her head.

I hate it. I hate the way she's looking at me, like I'm some puzzle she needs to solve. So, I do what I always do. I shut it down.

"I'm fine," I say flatly, setting the cup down again, this time softer.

"Yeah." Hazel snorts. "And I'm a master farmer."

"You're not."

"Exactly. And you're definitely *not* fine." She crosses her arms, one brow lifting. "So what's going on with you?"

"Jesus, Hazel." The bluntness nearly makes me choke on my coffee.

"What? If you're going to lie, at least try to sell it a little better."

I exhale sharply, my patience wearing thin. "You don't know what you're talking about."

"I think you canceled your supply run because you're hurting. You just told me thirty minutes ago you were done for the day because you had this run." Her voice softens, losing some of its usual fire. "I know you don't want to talk about it. But I also know pain when I see it."

Something about the way she says it sends a jolt through me. She doesn't look smug. Or nosy. She looks *concerned*. And I don't know what to do with that.

I try to get up. The pain flares hard and sharp, lancing through my knees and hands like hot wires. My vision tunnels for a second, black spots creeping at the edges. I lock my jaw, breathing through it, willing my body to cooperate.

I don't let my face show a damn thing. But Hazel is already on her feet.

"Beau—"

"I said I'm *fine*." It comes out harsher than I mean it to, but I don't take it back.

Her lips press together, her hands curl at her sides. For a second, I think she's going to push.

But then, she just shakes her head. "Right. Okay."

She takes a long sip of her coffee, then turns toward the door.

I should feel relieved. Instead, I just feel *tired*.

Before stepping outside, she stops and tosses one last look over her shoulder. "You can pretend all you want, but I'm not blind. And I don't buy your bullshit."

"Noted." I glare at her.

She smirks, like she knows she's under my skin.

Then she's gone, the door shutting behind her, leaving me alone with my aching joints and the lingering scent of coffee.

I sink into my chair and sigh.

She sees too much.

Most folks don't see anything at all. Not really. They think rheumatoid arthritis is just sore hands or maybe a little limp on a bad day. They don't see the way it steals things from you slowly—quiet and relentless. The way it makes you doubt your own body. Makes you feel like a damn imposter in your own skin.

They think if I'm upright, I must be fine. If I'm working, I must be strong.

But they don't know what it's like to wake up every morning and wonder which part of you won't work right today. Or to carry the weight of your legacy—land, labor, history—and know your body's slipping out from under it.

They don't see the toll.

I press my thumb into the swollen joint at the base of my hand, wincing.

Maybe Hazel's right. Maybe I am full of it.

But I don't know how to be anything else.

∼

I tell myself I'm making the supply run because it needs to be done. Not because Hazel got under my skin. Not because her voice is still rattling around in my head, full of stubborn concern and sharp-edged questions. Just because the farm needs things. *That's it.*

My hands don't want to grip. My knees don't want to bend. But I force them to.

Because if I stop, if I let myself sit too long, the pain settles in like roots in hard ground, and I won't be able to move at all.

And I sure as hell won't give Hazel the satisfaction of being right.

I load up the truck, drive into town, and ignore the way my body protests every bump in the road.

The supply store isn't too busy when I pull up. Good. The fewer people who see me like this, in this flare, the better.

I swing down from the truck, and my knees snap like old timber. Pain shoots through, sharp enough to steal my breath, but I suck it in and limp inside. Keep my head low. Get what I came for.

The first stretch of the run goes smooth enough—until I hit the chicken feed bags.

They're lined up neatly, waiting. Heavy as sin. A shiver of unease runs through me. I've lifted these a thousand times, easy as breathing. But today my arms hang like dead weight, thick and slow, fingers already twitching with the threat of letting go. Just the thought of crouching has my knees howling.

I grit my teeth. Ask for help? Not a chance.

I square my shoulders, pull in a breath, and drop into a crouch. Fire lances through my joints, white-hot and merciless, like someone's struck a match inside my bones. My teeth grind. Sweat beads at my hairline. I hook my hands under the first sack, the rough burlap biting into my palms, and heave.

For half a heartbeat, I've got it. The bag rises, heavy but

manageable, my muscles straining like frayed rope. My knees shake. My grip slips.

The bag thuds back to the concrete, a low, dull sound that echoes louder in my chest than in the store. My palms burn. My breath saws out of me, ragged.

I straighten slowly, swallowing down the noise of it. The ache in my back pulses like a warning light. I check around for witnesses. The aisle is empty, but humiliation still crawls under my skin.

Another breath. Another try. My fingers flex, reluctant.

"Come on," I growl to myself, low and fierce, as though the words might stiffen my spine. "Just one bag. One damn bag."

I crouch again, slower this time, lining up every joint, every inch of leverage I can steal. Pain blooms bright, hot, then steadies into a cold, mean throb. My hands clamp onto the burlap. My arms lock. My legs tremble, but hold.

The bag inches up, and up, my breath coming in hard bursts. Sweat slides down my temple. My vision blurs. But this time I don't drop it.

This time, I get it onto my shoulder.

For a heartbeat, victory swells—messy and hard-earned. My body's a battlefield, but I'm still standing on it. Still hauling feed. Still refusing to fold.

"Beau?"

I recognize the voice before I even look up.

I close my eyes a beat, try to shove the pain back down, and push myself upright. Too quick. Lightning bolts down my spine, but I grit through it, school my face into something neutral before I meet her gaze.

She's standing a few feet away, grocery bag dangling from one hand, eyes narrowing like she's caught me red-handed.

"What exactly are you doing?"

"What's it look like?" I nudge the feed bag at my boots.

Her mouth curves, not quite a smile. "Well, from here? I see a man in a wrestling match with a sack of corn."

"Thanks for the observation." My scowl only makes her grin.

"You're welcome. Free of charge." She tips her head, eyes flicking between my hands and my face. "You're hurt."

"I'm *fine*."

She lets out a laugh that says she doesn't believe me for a second. "You keep saying that like repetition is gonna rewrite reality. You cancelled today. Why are you here?"

I ignore her, crouching again. *Why is she here?*

"For God's sake—" She groans, exasperated. Then drops her grocery bag, marches forward, and grips the sack like it owes her money. With a noise somewhere between a war cry and a wheeze, she lifts it up, arms trembling, but somehow—she gets it into the truck bed.

I stand frozen, muscles slackening, memorizing how this slip of a woman does what I just failed to manage.

She turns back, brushing hair from her face. "There."

"You're going to hurt yourself."

"Oh, *I'm* going to hurt *myself*?" She gives me a look, hands on her hips. "You nearly *collapsed* trying to lift it."

"Did not."

"Did too."

Her grin softens, a flash of something new breaking through her sass. And damn it, I feel the corner of my mouth twitch. Just a little.

Then Hazel's shoulders drop. She steps closer, lowering her voice. "Beau . . . You don't have to prove anything."

I stiffen. "I'm not."

But the lie tastes sour on my tongue.

She tilts her head, eyes narrowing just a little, like she can see right through me. Always too sharp for her own good.

Why won't I just tell her? Hell, why won't I tell anybody straight?

The whole town already knows anyway. That's the curse of Maple Hollow—gossip runs hotter than summer asphalt, and it always finds its way back. Especially when it's about me. Born here. Raised here. The Rosewood boy who never left. The one who stayed behind, dragging the orchard with me while everyone else took off for bigger things.

They *know*.

But it's one thing to let people whisper about your stiff gait or the way you wince when lifting something heavy. It's another thing to *name it*.

Naming it makes it real. Naming it means it owns me. And I can't afford that.

Not with this land. Not with this legacy.

I was raised on pride and calluses, on the idea that you work through the pain, you don't talk about it. You sure as hell don't *ask* for help. My Pa didn't, my grandpa didn't. They worked themselves into the ground and wore that like a badge of honor.

And me? I'm the last one standing between this place and the dirt swallowing it whole.

So no, I don't want to tell her. Not because I think she'd mock me. Hell, she'd probably understand better than most. If I admit it . . . What am I supposed to be then?

I glance back at her. Hazel, with her messy determination, wild ideas, and soft heart. She doesn't get it yet—what it means to *belong* to land. To feel the weight of generations in your bones and know your body's betraying you anyway.

She gives me that same knowing look she always does. The one that makes me want to turn and walk away before she gets too close.

But I don't. Because I'm hurting. Because I'm tired. Because, for some reason, I don't actually *hate* the way she's looking at me. Like she cares. Like she's not going anywhere.

Hazel reaches out as if she's going to touch my arm, then

seems to think better of it. Instead, she just shakes her head and steps back.

We finish loading the last of the feed bags in silence, the tension from before hanging in the air like dust motes caught in a slow, shimmering drift. I can't shake the feeling that Hazel is somehow more attentive now, keeping track of every little twitch of my shoulders, every slight grimace when I shift my weight. I don't like it. And yet, I'm tired. Tired of being the grumpy, mean guy everyone expects me to be.

Her truck tails behind mine as we bump along the gravel back to the orchard.

"So, this is where the magic happens, huh?" she calls over the cab, practically flinging herself from her truck like a leaf caught in the wind.

I chuckle under my breath, rolling my eyes. "If by magic, you mean a lot of noise, a few smelly eggs, and occasional chaos, then sure. Magic."

"Aw, come on!" she protests, her grin broad enough to make the sun jealous. "How hard can it be? Just toss some feed and they'll go crazy!"

I shake my head, trying not to smile too openly. "Fine. Magic it is." I gesture toward the coop, where the chickens are pecking indifferently at their usual ration. "Here's how it works. Even though they have their feeders, I like to do this . . . "

I scoop a handful of feed, tossing it into the coop. The chickens flap, cluck, and squawk, turning the simple gesture into a chaotic ballet. Hazel's eyes widen, and she lets out a little laugh.

"Easy peasy!" she says, practically vibrating with excitement. "Let me try!"

I hand her the scoop. She approaches the coop with an exaggerated sense of ceremony. "Watch and learn, Beau!"

And then—chaos.

She tosses the feed a little too enthusiastically. Grain erupts into the air like a golden cloud, chickens squawking in delight and alarm. A few scatter into the corners, feathers flying. Hazel laughs, an unrestrained, melodic sound that ricochets against the barn walls. I stop for a moment, frozen, because . . . it's bright. It's infectious. And, dammit, it's catching.

"Look at them go! It's like a feathered tornado!" she squeals.

I snort, can't help it. "Tornado? More like a clucking disaster."

Her laugh makes me shake my head, amusement creeping in where annoyance used to live. She mimics the chickens' frantic movement, arms flapping like wings, voice pitched high. "Hey there, little buddy! You want some feed? C'mon!"

I nearly trip over my own boots from snickering. The sound of my own laugh, rough and unexpected, feels foreign. Like an old coat I hadn't worn in years. Hazel turns, her eyes wide, genuinely surprised.

"Did I just . . . make you laugh?" she asks softly.

"Yes," I admit, still grinning. "And it was . . . ridiculous."

"Exactly! Ridiculous is my specialty."

The chickens, now thoroughly entertained, scramble over the spilled feed, and Hazel claps her hands in triumph. The look on her face, bright and unrestrained, makes my heart clench. Not in pain. Something else. Something I haven't allowed myself in a long time.

She stands, brushing her hands off, and the loose strands slipping from her bun glow a pale rose-gold. She's oblivious to it, of course, wrapped up in her own tiny victory. I let her be.

"Just, don't get used to the nice guy, I am still the gruff one you see most of the time."

She laughs again, the kind that makes you wonder how the same person can carry so much light in such a small body.

I take her in for a moment longer, still clutching my scoop, still sneaking smiles when she isn't looking. The day feels a little warmer. The barn smells of feed and hay, but there's this brightness too.

Hazel

THE WALL

I've been in Maple Hollow a few weeks, and I pictured myself further along, but the early heat is already bearing down on me as I tug at a stubborn root, sweat trickling down my neck. My hands are covered in dirt, my hair is a tangled mess, and I probably look like I've been dragged through a hedge backward because I *have*.

Or rather, I've been waging war against the overgrown mess that used to be the flower beds of Pine & Petal.

I give one final yank, and the root snaps free, sending me stumbling backward. My foot catches on something—a broken piece of fence hidden in the weeds—and before I can stop myself, I go down hard.

Pain flares up my palm, sharp and stinging. I hiss, jerking my hand back, only to see a fresh slice running across my skin, already welling with blood.

"Oh, *come on*!" I groan, cradling my hand.

I sit there for a long moment, surrounded by the remnants of my battle with nature.

"What the hell was I thinking?" I whisper under my breath, shaking my head. "I should be in an air-conditioned office right now, drinking an overpriced latte and answering emails."

I squeeze my eyes shut, pressing the heel of my uninjured hand against my forehead.

I don't belong here.

I don't know what I'm doing.

I—*No*.

I inhale deeply, the smell of earth and fresh greenery grounding me. I *chose* this. I wipe my hand against my jeans, smearing dirt and blood together, and push myself up.

By midday, I've cleared a patch big enough to convince myself progress exists. The flower beds are still wild, but not entirely feral. A few blooms peek out between the carnage—zinnias, marigolds, stubborn little survivors who don't seem to care that I've been butchering their neighbors with reckless abandon.

I crouch beside a cluster of bright orange petals. "You're definitely flowers," I murmur. "Probably. Hopefully." Then I eye the green spiky thing crouched beside them. "But you—are you friend or foe?"

It's ridiculous, holding a staring contest with weeds, but at this point, my standards for sanity are low. I pluck one suspicious stalk and immediately regret it when milky sap oozes onto my already filthy fingers. "Ew. Okay, that feels hostile. You're a weed."

A small groan escapes me as I wipe my hands on my jeans, which have long since given up any pretense of being clothing and are now permanent rags.

My gaze drifts toward the back of the field, where weeds and wildflowers tangle into one indistinguishable mess. The fence line there is partially collapsed, the boards sagging like drunk old men, and the skeletal remains of floral wire dangle uselessly from their nails. It looks like a haunted graveyard for zinnias, and yet—there's something stubbornly hopeful about the few stems still clinging upright, their bright painted faces turn stubbornly toward the sun.

I step carefully between the rows, singing encouragement to the flowers like some eccentric plant coach. "You're doing great, sweeties. Don't mind me, just passing through."

My boot nudges a fallen fence post, and before I can step back, my shin catches on a loop of rusted floral wire. "Oh no. No, no, no."

I try to free myself, but the more I wiggle, the worse it gets. One loop tightens around my ankle, another snags my jeans, and then I trip sideways, catching my elbow on the fence post. I grunt, twisting, only to discover the wire now wrapped around my other foot.

"Seriously? Am I in some slapstick comedy?"

I attempt a graceful step forward, which results in a spectacular flail backward. My arms pinwheel, my hair whips into my face, and I land squarely on my rear end in a patch of thistles.

"Ow!" I yelp, jerking upright, only to discover the wire has me tethered like a goat on a short leash. I glare at the sagging fence, heat prickling up my neck. "I am being bullied by wood and string. This is a new low."

I attempt to wriggle free again, but every movement digs me deeper. Somewhere in the distance, a bird trills like it's laughing at me. "Yeah, yeah, very funny," I say, slightly panicked. "Nature is cruel."

Eventually, I go still, letting out a breath that sends a strand of sweaty hair flying from my cheek. My back aches, my hands sting, and I feel utterly ridiculous. And then— because apparently I've lost all control over my emotional responses—I start laughing. Big, snorting, can't-catch-my-breath laughter, the kind that rolls through me until my eyes water. I laugh so hard my cheeks hurt, and I end up collapsing sideways in the dirt, a muddy, tangled mess.

It's either laugh or cry, and I've already done both today.

After what feels like an eternity, I manage to untangle myself by sheer stubbornness and some very undignified crawling. I stagger upright, covered in mud and debris, hair sticking out at odd angles. If anyone saw me right now, they'd call for professional help.

By the time I limp back toward the house, the sun is slipping low, the sky soft streaks of peach and lavender. My muscles protest with every step, and when I finally make it to my room, I collapse face-first onto the bed without bothering to clean up first.

It's dark when I roll onto my back, aching in places I didn't know could ache. I fumble for my journal on the nightstand, the pages already smudged with dirt from previous entries. My hand trembles as I write, but the words come anyway.

If this is going to work, I need to start small.

I stare at the sentence for a long time, the ink still drying, my heart heavy but steady. Maybe I don't need to conquer the whole field in one day. Maybe I just need to take it one stubborn root, one broken fence post, one messy step at a time.

That used to terrify me, but now, it is almost relieving.

Beau

QUIET OBSERVATION

The bathroom light flickers when I flip it on, a soft amber glow over the worn tile and mirror. I strip off my shirt, the fabric clinging to my skin, damp from sweat and the lingering heat of the day's work.

My shoulders ache from hauling lumber, and there's a bruise blooming across my forearm from when the hammer slipped. Not that the chicken coop cares. Or the chickens, for that matter.

What I hadn't planned on was one of the hens limping when I went out this morning. At first, I thought she'd just snagged her foot in the wire, but when I knelt down, I spotted it—swollen, hot to the touch. Bumblefoot. Not exactly on my to-do list.

I spend the morning crouched in the dirt as I cleaned her up. She squawked like I was murdering her, wings flapping, claws raking my wrist. But I got the wound drained and wrapped, talking to her the way my mom used to. Gentle, steady. "Easy, girl. You'll be alright."

It's strange, the way the smallest things can take the biggest chunk of your day. I meant to replace the warped boards on the west side of the coop, but by the time the hen was bandaged and settled, the morning had already turned sweltering, the air dense and soupy around me.

Still, looking out later and seeing her perched with the others, pecking away like nothing happened—it settles something in me. Maybe all the sweat and the cursing and the splinters are worth it.

I catch a glimpse of myself in the mirror—broad shoulders sloping under the weight of too many years of work, arms lined with muscle and fatigue. There are calluses on my palms and bruises on my shins. My body's a roadmap of effort.

The hot water sputters to life, steaming almost instantly. I step in, hissing when it hits my shoulders. But I don't move. I let it pour over me, scorching and relentless, washing away the ache buried deep in my joints. My head drops forward, forehead resting against the cool tile, water streaming down my back in rivulets.

The tension in my muscles starts to ease, bit by bit. My hands uncurl from the fists they've been stuck in all day. I roll my neck, and it cracks with a sharp pop that makes me groan, simultaneously relieving and aching.

I drag a hand through my hair, soap slicking over my skin, the scent of cedar and clean earth greeting me. My breathing comes back to calm, and for the first time today, I let myself feel the weight of it all. The burn in my knees, the dull throb in my wrists. The frustration. The pride. The loneliness.

Oh, the loneliness.

The heat seeps into places nothing else can touch, behind my ribs, under my skin, down to the parts of me I don't show anyone.

Just for a moment, I forget the orchard, the arthritis, the woman with sharp eyes and stubborn hands who's taken root in the corner of my thoughts.

I just let myself feel.

And when the water finally runs cold, I stay a little longer, because here, in the quiet, under the spray, I'm not a man trying to hold himself together.

I'm just a man.

Forcing myself out of the shower, I dry off, avoiding the mirror.

I ease down onto the edge of the bed with a grunt, rubbing absently at my wrist. Hazel doesn't know. She sees something, sure, but she doesn't *know*.

I don't need her, or anyone, looking at me like I'm something fragile.

I stretch out, wincing as I settle against the mattress. The window is cracked open, letting in the cool night air, and from a distance, I swear I can hear the faintest hum of movement from Hazel's place.

She's still awake.

The thought shouldn't weigh on me the way it does. I roll over, shutting my eyes, forcing myself to push it all away. The day's done. Tomorrow will come. And whatever this is, it'll pass. It has to. Or I'll be damned.

The alarm buzzes like a mosquito in my ear, and I swat at it before rolling onto my side with a groan.

I swing my legs over the edge of the bed and sit for a moment, elbows on my knees, palms rubbing at my face like I can scrub the fatigue off. The room is still dim—wood-paneled walls painted a warm tobacco brown, with old curtains that never quite block out the sun but soften it into something honey-colored. The bed creaks as I stand, and the floor's cool under my feet, creaky in all the same places it's creaked since I was a boy.

I shuffle into the kitchen. It's not much—just a farmhouse kitchen like any other. Cabinets I built with my father, all knotted pine and worn handles. A table that's more scar than surface. There's a small mug waiting by the sink, and I fill it with the coffee that's already brewed, thanks to the old timer I finally remembered to set last night.

The first sip is bitter and perfect. I stare out the window as the world slowly wakes. Mist curls low over the orchard, wrapping around the trunks like it's reluctant to let the night go. The trees sway gently, still damp with dew, sunlight cutting through the fog in ribbons. The barn roof glints with morning condensation, and somewhere in the distance, a rooster crows like it owns the damn county.

I eat a quick breakfast—toast with blackberry jam, nothing fancy—and pop two anti-inflammatories with the second half of my coffee. My joints aren't loosened up yet, but I've got work to do.

In the bedroom, I pull on a clean flannel, soft with age, and jeans that are already streaked with dirt from yesterday's repairs. My boots go on last—heavier than they used to feel—and I shrug into my old canvas jacket before stepping outside.

The porch groans under my weight. I built this one myself a decade back, wide enough to sit on in the evenings with a beer and a good view of the fields. The wood's worn smooth now, paint long gone in some places, but it holds.

And as I stretch, trying to coax my body into cooperation, my eyes drift—unbidden—toward Hazel's place.

She's already out there.

Even from here, I can see the way she moves—determined, even when she's clearly dead on her feet. The dark smudges under her eyes say she didn't sleep much, but that doesn't stop her. She's hacking away at the mess of overgrowth near the fence line, brow furrowed, mouth set in a stubborn line.

She's got no business doing half the things she's doing with the kind of energy she's running on. And yet, she keeps going.

I walk out to the edge of my property, reclining against the fence post, the rough wood digging into my shoulder. My mouth works before my better sense catches up.

"You're gonna burn yourself out."

The words come out rougher than I mean them.

Her head snaps up, eyes flashing across the distance between us. "I don't need a lecture, Beau."

The defensive bite in her tone hits harder than I expect. She wipes at her forehead with the back of her hand, glaring like I just told her she couldn't do it at all.

I bit back what I could say. That she's got more guts than most people I've met. That I know exactly what it's like to work yourself to the bone because the thought of stopping feels worse than the ache in your body.

Because I see myself in her. Younger, cockier, convinced sheer willpower could outrun exhaustion. Back before I learned the hard way that stubbornness can break you just as quickly as it can build you.

But encouragement? That's not something I'm good at. Not anymore.

I shove my hands deeper in my pockets, force my gaze back toward the orchard. "Suit yourself," I say firmly, shutting it down before anything else slips out.

When I peer back, she's already turned away, shoulders tight, swinging that spade like she's determined to prove me wrong.

And maybe she will.

I take the long way through the orchard. This place has always been my sanctuary. It's work, sure, but it's *my* work.

Something steady. Something I understand.

I run my hand over the rough bark of one of the older apple trees, feeling the years worn into it. This tree's been around longer than I have, rooted deep, unshaken by storms or seasons. Some days, I wish I felt that solid.

The thought sticks with me as I get to pruning, working

slowly, carefully, like my body isn't screaming at me to take it easy.

Halfway through filling a basket with cut branches, I hear the crunch of tires on gravel. Mama's truck rolls up the drive, kicking up dust, her silhouette clear in the driver's seat. I wipe my hands on my jeans, already bracing myself as she parks, steps out, and gives me *the look*.

Lord help me.

"You been eatin' right?" she asks, skipping a greeting altogether.

"Morning to you, too, Mama."

"Don't 'morning' me." She narrows her eyes. "You look tired."

I glance back at the orchard, avoiding her stare. "Just keeping up with the work."

"Mm-hmm. And the work's gonna keep up with *you* right into an early grave if you don't start listening to your body."

I look over to Hazel, kicking myself for my own karma. There's no point arguing when she's like this. Instead, I do the smart thing—I walk over, kiss her cheek, and take the bag she's holding before she can swat me with it.

She sniffs, clearly unimpressed with my attempts at distraction.

"I brought you some soup. And cornbread."

Peeking inside the bag, I say, "You tryna fatten me up?"

She smacks my arm. "I'm trying to make sure my son doesn't live off coffee and stubbornness."

I don't argue, because honestly? She's not wrong.

We settle onto the porch. She asks about the orchard, the harvest, the market. I answer, easy enough, until she shifts in her seat and gives me a knowing look.

"So . . ."

I pause mid-sip of my coffee. ". . . So?"

"How's the new neighbor?" She smirks.

Lord help me twice.

"Fine." I keep my expression neutral.

"Just fine?"

"Yup." I take another slow sip.

She observes me for a second longer before sighing and standing. "Alright, I won't pry. But eat the damn soup."

"Yes, ma'am."

She heads back to her truck, shaking her head.

"I forgot something," she says, voice lighter than usual, but there's a tension under it. The kind that says she's thought this through, and she's gonna say it no matter how I look at her. She puts her hand out, a small tin resting in her palm.

"That so?" I raise an eyebrow.

"Salve. Made it with Miss Loretta last week. Arnica, cayenne, turmeric, a touch of comfrey. And don't you roll your eyes at me, Beau Daniel Rosewood—I *know* that look."

"You think I'm gonna rub chili pepper on my knees?" I look at it like it might bite me.

Ma rolls her eyes. "It's not that kind of cayenne. It warms. Helps with inflammation. And if you're too proud to try it, you can at least lie and say it smells nice."

"I'm fine," I lie, knowing I've already lost.

"You're *proud*," she corrects. "Not fine. And you're too damn stubborn to ask for help, even from people who care."

"Ain't nobody else's business," I grunt, still not looking at her.

Mama's quiet for a beat. Then she hums, not unkindly. "I know you think that. I do. But pain don't go away just 'cause you keep it to yourself. You think no one notices? This town's small, Beau. People talk."

"They always talk."

"They do," she agrees, nudging the tin back toward me when I start to set it down. "But not always outta cruelty. Some of us talk because we love you. Jonas said you haven't called him back."

I stiffen. "I don't need Jonas."

She sighs, softer now, like she's tired of fighting this same fight with me. "Jonas *gets it*. He's not gonna coddle you or pity you. He'll just show you what works and what doesn't. You're not weak for having a bad day, Beau. You're human. Your Pa . . . he pushed himself far beyond his capabilities, and now, look, we are without him."

"I don't want to talk about it."

Mama doesn't flinch. She rests her hand briefly over mine—the one still holding the tin—and gives it a light pat.

"Alright, baby. Then don't. Just promise me you'll use that salve. And if you *do* call him, maybe don't wait 'til you can't get outta bed to admit you need something."

I nod, because it's all I can manage.

She smiles, presses a kiss to the top of my head like she did when I was a kid, and stands.

"Eat your soup. And take care of that damn body of yours. It's the only one you've got."

She walks back to her truck, leaving behind the scent of lavender and sass and too many truths I'm not ready to face.

I sit there a long time after she's gone, the salve warm in my hand.

Still, I don't call Jonas.

But I don't throw the salve away either.

I look over at Hazel one more time, and for some reason, I am smiling.

Hazel

FIRST SUCCESS

I push my nearly empty cart through Maple Hollow's only grocery store, scanning the shelves with growing regret. The small-town charm I once found so quaint is working against me now. This isn't like Seattle, where I could walk into a store at any hour and find exactly what I need. Nope—here, if I don't time my grocery run right, I'm left digging through slim pickings and trying to figure out how to make a meal out of a can of beans, an onion, and whatever mystery meat is left in the butcher's case.

I spend all morning elbow-deep in the flower beds, gardening book in one hand, pruning shears in the other, like some kind of wannabe Martha Stewart on caffeine. Turns out most of the plants already in the beds aren't weeds like I thought. *Sorry, innocent greenery!*

I pause in front of a display of flour and sugar, chewing my lip. Do I want to start baking? No. Do I want to eat anything that doesn't come from a microwave or the questionable contents of my fridge? Yes.

I groan and grab a bag of flour. Then, just as I turn the corner, my phone vibrates. I peek at the screen—and instantly wish I hadn't. *Liam.*

Do I answer this?

I stare at the name, my finger hovering over the decline button. I should ignore it. I *should*. But before I can stop myself, I swipe to accept.

"Hello?"

A beat of silence. Then—

"Hazel."

His voice is the same. Deep. Familiar. A little too smooth.

I grip the cart. "What do you want?"

Another pause. "You haven't returned my calls."

"There's a reason for that." I give myself a pat on the back for sounding firm, grabbing a fresh container of cinnamon to replace the radioactive one in my pantry.

"Come on, Haze. We don't have to do this." He exhales, like *I'm* the frustrating one.

"Do what, exactly?" A bitter laugh escapes me. "Pretend you didn't completely screw me over?" A girl wanders into the aisle, black hair hanging in her face like a curtain. Instead of giving me the judgment I expect, she offers a look that's almost sympathetic. Then she mouths one word—*boys*—like it's something she's said a hundred times before. I suppress a giggle.

"That's not fair."

"Liam, why are you calling me?"

"I just . . ." He hesitates. "I wanted to check in. See how you're doing."

Liar. I know him too well. I know when he's playing his cards, when he's putting on that concerned act to make himself feel better. And I won't be a part of it.

"You lost the right to check in on me," I say quietly. "I don't need you, Liam."

Another stretch of silence. I poke a bag of powdered sugar, and a small cloud of refined dust escapes the corner. I gently add it to my cart.

Then, softer, "You really staying out there?"

"Yes."

"You sure that's where you belong?"

His words hit deep. Because the truth is—I *don't* know. Not really. I'm still figuring it out. Still trying to prove to myself that I can do this. But I'll be damned if I admit that to him.

So I force my voice steady. "Yes, Liam. I'm sure." I end the call before he can say anything else.

And then I set my phone back in my pocket, press my hands to the cart, and let out a shaky breath. I won't cry. I *won't*.

Liam was my high school sweetheart . . . and my coworker. In the end, he didn't just break my heart—he took my job too.

We had history, the kind that wraps around your bones and lingers in the quiet moments when you think you're alone. He was the boy who used to kiss my forehead like I was something delicate, who held my hand under cafeteria tables, who promised me forever when we were seventeen and foolish enough to believe in it.

But life had a way of wearing us down. Somewhere between graduation and the real world, between long shifts and exhaustion, between his dreams and mine, we stopped being a team. I wanted stability. He wanted something else—something I could never quite hold on to. He changed, or maybe I did. Or maybe we both just realized that love alone wasn't enough.

We tried. God, we tried. But it was never the same. I would catch him looking at me like I was something heavy, something dragging him down. And when I finally asked him if he still loved me, he hesitated. So I left. That was the only thing I ever gave up on. But that was because he gave up on me—on *us*.

And then, months later, he came back—apologizing, wanting another chance, swearing that he had made a mistake. And maybe he had. But so had I, every time I let him back in, every time I believed that the boy I loved still existed in the man he had become.

Today, I'm done.

I pull out my phone, my fingers hovering over his name for just a moment before I block his number. A finality settles over me, heavy but right. I set my phone down.

"I won't think about him again," I whisper, my voice barely audible over the store sounds. Never again.

The aisle does not answer. But somehow, I know it heard me.

When I get home, I waste no time throwing the groceries into their spots in a rush to get out in the fields before night rolls in.

I throw my hair up in a bun, wiggle out of my leggings into my rags—I mean jeans—and toss on a flannel I found at the local second-hand store.

Returning to the patchwork mess I squat low, letting my hands wander through the tangled stems. I've passed them a hundred times since I got here, but today . . . today I feel a little spark of something. A little spark that whispers—maybe I can make something beautiful, maybe I can give a piece of this place to someone else.

I've never done this before—never made bouquets for anyone. What if I mess it up? What if it looks silly? What if no one cares? A hush catches in my throat as I lift up a zinnia, its petals still stubbornly upright despite the weeds that tried to swallow it. I tuck it gently in my lap, then pause to study it. It's simple. It's alive. It's hopeful.

Okay. Maybe I can do this.

I start slow, gingerly picking a few more flowers. Marigolds, some daisies, a sprig of lavender that smells faintly of late summer and earth. I hold them together, turning them in my hands, trying to see what feels right. It's awkward. Stems slip, petals bend the wrong way. I frown.

"Not too bad," I murmur, but the words feel hollow. I start

again, more deliberately, testing each stem before adding it, layering colors, feeling the textures beneath my fingertips.

The string is another problem. I rummage through the shed and find a coil of twine, frayed at the ends but strong enough. I tug a length free and sit cross-legged, fumbling with the bundle as I try to wrap it neatly. It slides, awkwardly, stubbornly, but finally, I twist a clumsy knot that somehow holds everything together. I ease back, hands dirty, and stare.

It's not perfect. Some stems stick out at odd angles. Some petals are tattered. But it's alive, and it feels like *mine*. A small, shy thrill curls through my chest. I never thought I could make something like this. I never thought I'd dare.

I hug the first bouquet to me like it's a treasure, spinning slightly on the spot, imagining a face lighting up when it's handed over. My stomach does a little flip. Should I give it to someone I know? Someone kind? Maybe Lody at the bookstore—always so kind, always buried in her stacks of books. Or the diner, where the smell of fresh coffee and toast makes everything feel brighter. I bite my lip. Saffron. Maggie. Who deserves the first little burst of joy?

A laugh escapes me when a petal falls to the dirt. I brush it off and set the bouquet carefully on the grass beside me, crouching to start the second one. The rhythm is slower now, gentler. I layer blooms, test stems. Each bouquet becomes its own little creature, full of color and scent, a little messy, a little stubborn, and utterly alive.

By the time I finish the third, my hands ache, my knees are stiff, and my hair sticks to my neck. But I feel light, almost giddy. I hold a bouquet up to the sky, the petals catching the light, and my grin stretches wide. I made something with my own hands, something meant to bring someone else joy.

I tuck a sprig of lavender behind my ear and step toward the home, carrying the first bouquet like a secret treasure. My heart flutters. Whoever gets this doesn't know it yet, but I do. Today is the first day of all the days I've been imagining.

I pass the truck and decide to walk. I slip the first bouquet under my arm and step onto the dusty road leading into town. My boots crunch over gravel, each step sending a tiny thrill up my spine. The air smells of warm asphalt, and as I pass Beau's orchard, the faintest smell of apples. I let my eyes drift and see Beau on the swing out back. He is sitting alone, and a small part of me feels bad for him. But only a small part.

The bookstore is first. I push open the door, and the little bell jingles, announcing me. Lody looks up from the counter, her glasses slipping down her nose as she frowns in concentration at a stack of returned books.

"Morning, Lody," I say, my voice steadier than I feel.

She glances at me, then down at the bundle of flowers. Her frown softens, curiosity flickering across her face.

"I . . . um . . . thought you might like these," I say, holding out the bouquet.

Her eyes widen, and for a moment she just stares. Then a smile spreads slowly, lighting her face in a way that makes me swell with warmth. She takes the flowers gently, inhaling the faint scent of lavender and marigold.

"Oh, Hazel . . . these are lovely," she says, voice soft. "Just . . . thank you. Truly."

The pride hits me like a wave. I never thought a few flowers could feel like a victory, but here it is, warm and buzzing.

I thank her and slip back onto the street, heart still skipping. The diner is only a block away. I push open the door and am greeted by the comforting smells of frying bacon and strong coffee. Saffron looks up from clearing a table, her eyes catching on the flowers in my hand.

"Well, hello there," she says, surprised. "What have we here?"

I hold out the bouquet, smiling shyly. "Thought it might brighten someone's morning."

Her grin spreads. "Hazel, these are beautiful. You made them?"

"Yeah," I admit, a little breathless. "I—well, I just picked what looked good."

"Looks good?" Her eyes sparkle. "Hazel, you've got a gift. These . . . they make everything feel lighter. Like the sun's sneaking in through the windows."

I feel a little child-like, and maybe a little reckless. I want to linger in the warmth of her reaction, but I have more blooms tucked under my arm. Still, I let myself savor this small triumph.

Later, walking back toward the edge of town, a couple of locals are lined against the fence by the square, chatting. One nudges the other, nodding in my direction. I catch the words, carried just loudly enough for me to hear.

"Beau is losing his bet."

I pause mid-step, a smirk tugging at my lips. I like that. I *really* like that.

My heart is full.

I can carve a little life here, one that's all my own, one messy, stubborn, joyful step at a time.

Beau

MEMORIES & PAIN

I step out of the barn, squinting against the morning sky greeting me. Hazel's out there again, kneeling low in the far field, hands buried in the dirt like she's waging war against the land. I shake my head, muttering under my breath. She doesn't need me hovering—doesn't need anyone hovering.

To the orchard I go, letting my eyes drift back to her one last time. And then—

I do a double-take.

Something about the way the flannel hugs her shoulders, the way it's soft and worn, the color catching the light . . .

I do a triple-take.

No. That can't be.

It *is*.

The flannel I donated weeks ago is wrapped around her. A knot forms in me, my hands curling into fists at my sides. The flannel—*my flannel*—on her. She looks completely unaware of its origin, completely alive in it, completely . . . impossibly distracting.

I grunt low, shaking my head. Focus, Beau. Just focus.

Except I don't. My eyes keep flicking back, drawn despite myself, and I realize the orchard, the morning, the sun—all of it—is suddenly irrelevant compared to the way she moves in a shirt that was once mine.

Lord.

I turn back to the orchard, forcing my gaze downward, letting the gentle warmth seep into my aching shoulders while my hands grip the pruning shears. *The flannel.* I shove the thought away, muttering about crooked branches and stubborn roots. Focus, Beau. Focus.

The orchard is quiet except for the creak of branches and the faint hum of insects. My hands ache as I prune, stiff joints reminding me of every year I've spent out here, every mistake Pa corrected when I didn't know better. I remember the time I cut too deep into a young apple tree, thinking I knew what I was doing, and Pa's voice cutting through the air like a whip.

"Beau, you'll kill it before it even grows. Hands, not haste."

I grimace at the memory. I've always carried that lesson with me, even if my pride sometimes forgets it.

I work slowly, deliberately, letting my body move in rhythm with the trees, hiding the pain as best I can.

Later, I'm on the porch, phone cradled to my ear, pretending to be irritated as Jonas's voice carries through the line.

"So . . . Hazel, huh?" I say, tone casual, clipped.

"Beau," Jonas chuckles. "I can hear the way you're talking. That's fascination, not annoyance."

"I'm just keeping tabs," I grunt. "Somebody's got to make sure she doesn't burn herself out."

"Uh-huh," Jonas teases. "Sure. That's why you're sneaking apples and gloves onto her porch."

I tighten my grip on the phone, regretting telling him, clearing my throat. "I'm . . . practical. For the farm."

"Right," Jonas says, knowing better. "You've been eyeing her. Admit it. There's something about her, isn't there?"

I freeze, letting silence answer for me. Tightness coils in

me, stubborn and reluctant. Jonas doesn't need more than that. He knows. He always knows.

Before I can concoct another excuse, the phone buzzes again. I frown at the screen. Gideon's grandson. I let Jonas go, mumbling something I tune out.

"Hey, Beau," comes the excited voice, all fast words and barely contained energy. "You gotta hear this—Hazel's brought bouquets into town. To the diner and the bookstore. Everyone's talking about them. And . . . Ma's home happy as a bee."

I sink back in my chair, trying not to let the twitch at the corner of my mouth betray anything. Hazel. Bouquets. People smiling. And Maggie . . . happy.

I run a hand over my face, feeling that tug of something I don't want to name. Pride? Admiration? Something more dangerous, something that makes me realize how much I've let myself shut down.

"Thanks," I say into the phone, voice quieter than usual. "I'll . . . I'll let her know you said that."

As I hang up, I look toward the fields again, imagining her there, flannel snug around her, hair tousled by the wind, that stubborn grin still in place.

That tug within me tightens, and I shake my head. Not her. Don't let it be her.

I've built walls high and thick, and with good reason. Too many people, too much care, and everything I've loved has been chipped away by circumstance, by sickness, by absence. I keep my distance because I know the cost. I keep my distance because I can't bear to let anyone in, not fully, not enough to get hurt again.

But still, my gaze keeps flicking back to where I imagine her kneeling, her hands working the soil, creating something bright and alive from nothing.

One cut at a time. One branch. One day. That's all I can manage. *One day at a time.*

THE STAND

I wake up, and the first thing I do is reach for my phone. It's still warm from charging overnight, and the screen lights up with notifications I don't bother checking yet. Instead, I scroll. PinBoard. My feed.

And somehow, someway, it's perfect. Exactly what I've been craving without even knowing it. Every pin is like a little window into my dream life. Flower-strewn farmhouses, tiny bookshops with plants spilling from every corner, sun-dappled porches, and yes . . . occasionally, a ridiculously handsome farmer working the fields. That impossible, delicious tightening hits me, like I've stumbled into someone else's story that just happens to feel exactly like mine.

I scroll past one picture after another, and then I stop. A flower stand. Not just any flower stand—a fully realized, organized, vibrant little paradise, with blooms stacked in baskets, little chalkboard signs, and petals spilling over the edges like they don't care about rules. My heart does a little skip.

I tilt my phone, zooming in, and beneath the main display, I notice the related pins. Smaller stands, more rustic setups, ways to tie bouquets with twine, ways to display flowers in milk jugs, tiny pots, and even old mason jars. Each one makes my mind race with possibilities.

As I sit up straighter, the blankets fall around me. Ideas tumble over each other in my head, little sparks of "maybe this" and "what if I try that." I bite the inside of my cheek, trying not to squeal at the possibilities, my fingers hovering over the screen as if touching it will somehow pull the inspiration straight into my hands.

Pushing off the covers, I grab my notebook from the bedside table. I've scribbled down a few ideas over the past week, but today, I feel like I can actually make them real. I shuffle into the kitchen, pouring a cup of tea to wake up fully, then wander outside to the shed where I've been stashing leftover flowers and supplies.

A warm sheen sweeps over the worn wood floor, highlighting bundles of marigolds, daisies, and lavender, some still wrapped in damp paper from last week. I pull out my notebook and flip to the page with the building plans for the stand. I trace the lines with my finger, feeling a thrill each time I see how simple it really is. Just a few steps—measurements, a couple of cuts, and some assembling. It's almost laughably doable. My body tightens with excitement.

I dig out my phone and place an online order for the lumber and hardware I'll need. Gideon's grandson will deliver it later in the day, but for now, I want to get my hands on the fun stuff. Mason jars, milk jugs, ribbons, chalkboards . . . the little touches that will make it feel like *my* stand.

Purse in hand, I head into town. The local second-hand store is a treasure trove, the kind of place that smells like polished wood and old paper, with shelves that groan under the weight of forgotten things. I spend what feels like hours sifting through jars of every size, ribbons that might have been used for gift wrap at one time, tiny chalkboards, and even a few rustic baskets that have clearly seen better days. A week ago, I found a flannel here—worn, soft, and just perfect—and

I can still remember the way it fit like it had been waiting for me.

Every time I find something that could work, I hold it up, imagining it at the stand. A jar brimming with fresh flowers, tied with a frayed ribbon, a chalkboard propped up with the day's offerings written in wobbly letters, or a milk jug spilling lavender into the open air. My heart races, and I can't help the small, almost manic laugh that escapes me.

By the time I'm done, my arms are full of loot, my bag heavy, but I don't even care. Back at the farmhouse, I spread everything across the kitchen table, stepping back to admire the chaos. My savings account is quietly screaming at me, dwindling faster than I expected, but it's worth it. If I can sell even a handful of bouquets, it'll all feel like treasure, like proof.

I sink into a chair, staring at the jars, ribbons, and flowers, letting the colors dance across petals and glass alike. I feel like I've planted a seed—not in soil, but in something bigger. My fingers hover over the marigolds, daisies, and lavender, tracing the curves of petals and imagining the bouquets they'll become.

I drag the hose over to the flower beds, tugging at the kinked end until water finally hisses through. The droplets hit the soil in a satisfying splash, darkening the earth, sending a fresh, earthy scent into the air. I kneel down, moving the nozzle in wide arcs, soaking every row, every stubborn weed I haven't gotten to yet. Water trickles down my back, cold against the warmth of the day, and I can't help but grin. It's messy. It's real. And I love it.

The rumble of a truck pulls me from my reverie. I squint, shielding my eyes, and sure enough—it's Gideon's grandson, his truck bed piled with lumber, screws, and hardware.

"Morning, Hazel!" he calls, hopping down. "Got your order."

I wipe my hands on my jeans and head over. "Perfect timing. Thanks for bringing it."

He eyes the hose. "Need a hand?"

"I'm good," I say, though the water has soaked the front of my shirt. I can do this.

"You sure?" He shifts from foot to foot. "Beau could help —he's good with this kind of thing."

I shake my head. "I've got it. Don't worry."

He grunts in protest, unloading the wood anyway. I follow, carrying boards to the little clearing I eyed for the stand. Every piece feels heavy in my hands, every nail and screw a small reminder that this isn't just a dream anymore.

I start putting the boards together, lining them up as best as I can. Hammer in hand, I work slowly, deliberately, my tongue peeking out between my teeth in concentration. I don't notice the slight wobble, the one upside-down board, until I step back and squint. "Well, that's new," I mutter to myself, laughing despite the minor frustration.

But it doesn't matter. I grab a brush and a can of paint. I still haven't tossed from the mud room clean-out. In shaky, uneven letters, I paint across the front.

Pine & Petal.

The brushstrokes aren't perfect, the letters wobble and tilt, but somehow it feels *right.*

The light catches on the painted letters, the freshly hammered boards, the flowers I've been gathering. I laugh softly, wiping at my cheeks. Who would have thought? Who would have guessed that all it would take to make me feel this alive was dirt under my nails, a crooked flower stand, and a handful of wild blooms?

I step back from the stand, brushing a strand of hair from my face and surveying my handiwork. The bouquets are arranged in jars and milk bottles, marigolds bright as captured fire, daisies soft and cheerful, lavender delicate and soothing, a random price is scribbled in chalk—something that feels right, but I'm not even sure if it's right at all. I pause, thinking of how I'll get people to notice. How will anyone even know these exist?

That is a tomorrow Hazel problem. I decide firmly. Tonight, I just need to savor this.

I check my phone. The weather looks decent, no rain forecasted. A slight breeze—perfect for leaving the flowers out without worrying too much. Feelings twirl around me, much anticipation and a little pride. For all the chaos, the trial-and-error, the dirt, sweat, and scrapes, this feels like magic.

Finally, I drag myself inside, shoes muddy, hair tangled, heart full. I flop onto the couch with my journal and a pen, the pages thick with scribbles, ideas, and random musings from the past weeks. I let the pen drift across the paper, recounting today's victories, such as the stand, the flowers, the way the paint smeared slightly but somehow added character, the giddy little thrill of imagining someone stopping by and smiling at my creations.

And then I can't resist. I reach for the old journal I found tucked in the closet when I was cleaning. I've already read a few entries, the one about the sign the most notable, but tonight, I flip to the next page.

June 14th

I never thought I'd find love here. Not the kind that knocks you off your feet, not the kind that comes with grand declarations and promises. I have that with Henry. No, I am talking about the kind I've found. It is quieter. Patient. It grows slowly, like the flowers in the garden, or the vegetables in the greenhouse.

I've learned to love my hands again, even when they're calloused and cracked. I've learned to love the hours spent alone in the sun, pulling weeds and pruning roses, because in those moments, I am tending to more than just plants. I am tending to myself.

I've learned that love doesn't have to be loud to matter. It's in the care I take with the soil, the way I remember which blooms are delicate and which are stubborn. It's in the pride that swells when a tiny bud opens into something beautiful. And it's in the patience to forgive myself when I get it wrong.

This farm has taught me that self-love isn't selfish. It's essential. And in loving myself here, I've opened my heart, not to someone else first, but to the life I never thought I could truly call my own.

Clara

I read it twice, then close the journal gently. My chest feels lighter, warmer, as if some invisible weight has shifted. If she could find that kind of love here—if she could claim it amidst soil and blooms and hard work—then I can too.

Morning rises, and a rooster crows somewhere on Beau's property.

I stretch, yawning, and pull myself toward the kitchen. Halfway through my toast, butter melting into the crumb, I catch a flicker of movement out of the corner of my eye.

Someone's at the stand. *Already?*

My fork drops with a clatter. My tea sloshes dangerously in its mug. Without thinking, I kick off my slippers, grab my robe, and sprint through the house, hair a tangled mess, robe flapping behind me like a banner of impending chaos.

"Good morning!" I yell before I even reach the porch, my voice cracking somewhere between excitement and disbelief.

"Mornin', Hazel!" Maggie's face lights up, all bright-eyed enthusiasm. She's crouched near the stand, holding the last bouquet. My heart thuds.

"You're buying the last one?" I gasp, skidding to a stop, hand hovering over the jars as if she might change her mind.

Maggie grins, nodding. "I wouldn't miss it. They're beautiful."

I spin around, scanning the stand frantically. "Were they . . . were they stolen? Did someone . . . ?"

"Nope," Maggie says with a laugh. "I heard from Saffron at the diner, and she heard from Lody at the bookstore, and she said Gideon's grandson mentioned it, and then Beau . . ." She pauses, eyes twinkling. "Beau told him. And here we are."

Beau. Somehow involved? Somehow, this tiny ripple of attention has traveled from him to the town. My mind shifts between big emotions—pride, disbelief, delight—all at once.

I grin, trying to steady my voice. "Well, I—wow. Thank you, Maggie. Really."

She laughs again, hoisting the bouquet with care. "I can't wait to show it off at the diner!"

As she walks off, I hear the crunch of boots on gravel, and the quiet hits me in a different way.

"Hazel," he says as he passes by, his voice low and gruff,

like he's not entirely comfortable letting his attention show. His eyes flick over the stand. "These prices. They might be a little low."

My eyes scan the little chalkboard, then back at him. "Maybe. But they're my first attempt at figuring it out."

He grunts, not exactly a concession, but his tense aura relaxes just a fraction. "You'll learn. Don't undersell yourself."

Something shifts in the line of his mouth, the angle of his shoulders. Pride? Or maybe just his mask slipping. I don't comment, don't say I know. I just nod, letting him walk on, the briefest moment of connection hanging between us.

I stand there a moment, looking at the empty jars and the crooked sign.

Success. Real success.

It isn't instant. It isn't flashy. It's persistence, it's showing up, it's learning along the way, it's letting small victories—like Maggie's smile and Beau's rare acknowledgment—carry you forward.

"Thank you," I say, softly.

He turns around, no words, just a small twinkle in his eye.

I swear I happy dance for a solid ten minutes before running back inside.

Sold out. Wow. Just . . . wow.

Hazel

PROJECT THANK-A-BEAU?

My phone buzzes in the middle of arranging a small stack of vases on a towel to dry. I wipe my finger on the corner of the towel and press accept, noting Mom's contact picture. I need to update it, it was from our 2015 Florida vacation.

"Hey, Mom."

"Hazel, honey, did you see the text I sent about your mail?" Her voice is brisk, the kind that makes me feel like I should already be on top of whatever she's about to launch into.

"Uh . . . no. Why? Did something come for me?" I keep rinsing, nonchalant.

"Yes! Can I open it?"

"Sure, sure. Open it," I say, holding up my hands like I'm surrendering. Not that she can see me.

There's a pause, then a little gasp from the other end. "Hazel! This . . . this is a job offer. For a senior lead analyst position at the corporation you interviewed with a year ago!"

I freeze mid-rinse, suds dripping from my fingers. "Wait—what? How—why now?"

Mom's voice softens slightly, like she's trying to soothe a startled child. "Looks like it got forwarded from your old address. Must've been sitting there a few months, even before you made your move. They didn't lose interest in you, it's just . . . delayed, apparently."

A strange little relief bubbles up in my chest. So, this isn't some new twist of fate, some sudden life-altering thing. It's old news catching up to me. Somehow, knowing that makes it feel less like pressure and more like a curiosity.

"Mom," I say, tucking a loose strand of hair behind my ear while rinsing another dish, "I . . . okay. Got it."

"No, Hazel. This is huge. This is the kind of opportunity that people dream about! Senior lead analyst! The experience, the prestige—think of the résumé, the networking, the—" She launches into a rapid-fire lecture of business jargon, each word fancier than the last.

I shrink a little, letting her rush past me, even with just words, like she always does. Nodding, murmuring small affirmations I don't even fully register. I feel the tug of her excitement, the weight of her expectations pressing against me.

"Hazel? Hello? You're not ignoring me, are you?"

"Not ignoring," I call back, my voice a little muffled by the soap bubbles clinging to my hands. "Just listening."

Mom lets out a long breath, triumphant and slightly exasperated. "Good. Just promise me you'll consider it seriously. I mean, this is everything you've worked for, and—"

I tune her out. And somehow, just for a moment, I feel okay. I don't have to decide right this second. The world won't collapse while I am out here building something new.

"Promise," I murmur, and she doesn't push any further. I hang up.

A slow smile spreads across my face. Fancy words, big corporate titles . . . they're not enough to shake the little farm life I'm carving out for myself. Not today.

I sank onto the kitchen stool, the hum of the refrigerator filling the stillness. Somewhere outside, a rooster crows—though never on cue. He seems to prefer his own schedule, turning it into a sort of guessing game. When would he decide the morning had officially begun?

The mail that has found me still sits in a neat little pile on the counter, untouched. I don't reach for it. Not yet.

Instead, I pull my laptop over, balancing it on the counter next to my tea. My fingers hover over the keys, hesitant at first, like I'm about to open some door I'm not sure I want to step through. I remember the way Maggie's eyes lit up when she picked up the last bouquet.

And I realize something. This little farm, these flowers, even the stumbles and failures along the way—they feel like me. Real me. The part of me I'd lost in spreadsheets and boardrooms and conference calls, the me that used to hide behind logic and numbers, the me that forgot how to breathe in color and sunlight. The me that heals from L—nope, not even giving him the dignity of saying his name.

I take a slow breath, steadying myself, and open a new spreadsheet. One sheet for blooms. One sheet for costs. One sheet for potential sales. I start typing—names of flowers, planting dates, harvest windows. Columns for ribbons, jars, chalkboard signs, and even the random odds and ends I pick up at the secondhand store.

Formulas I used to live and breathe in my corporate life flicker back into my mind—SUM, AVERAGE, IF statements. I smile, a small, secret smile. Who would've thought that everything I learned in high-rise offices and fluorescent-lit conference rooms could still matter here, in a field of dirt and wide-open brightness?

I track the costs of my tiny flower stand. Then I calculate the projected revenue if each bouquet sells for a few dollars. The numbers are modest. Tiny. But they're real. Tangible. And more importantly, they make sense. I can see a path forward without the stress and polish of corporate ambition suffocating me.

A chart emerges illustrating blooms versus cost, hours worked versus expected profit, and even a rough schedule for watering, pruning, and bouquet preparation. Each number, each cell, each line of color feels like a map, guiding me toward something I want—not something someone else expects of me.

I settle into my chair, sipping my tea, letting the quiet pride settle in. I feel capable. Not like I did in a boardroom, chasing KPIs that meant nothing to me, but capable in a way that matters. I can fail here, I can try again, and each misstep doesn't break me—it teaches me.

Tomorrow, I think, I'll figure out how to spread the word even farther. But today, I plan. Chart. Dream. And in this careful, deliberate blending of old skills and new life, I feel a thrill that's entirely mine.

By the time noon has found me, I've rinsed my teacup, tidied the kitchen, and tucked the spreadsheet neatly into a folder on my laptop home screen. The numbers are still there, waiting for me to return, but for now, I need something different. Something lighter.

I slip out to the porch, letting the warm air hit me, and press against the railing. From here, I can see the flower stand, a cheerful little patch of color against the gravel drive. And I can't stop thinking about what Maggie said yesterday—the trail of whispers that led all the way back to Beau.

Beau.

It doesn't surprise me that he kept his fingerprints off the kindness, not really. He's the type to tuck good deeds behind that scowl of his, to act like he's just "doing his duty." But I know the truth now. And the truth is, he's the reason anyone even stopped by Pine & Petal in the first place.

I chew my lip, wondering what to do about that. How do you thank a man who probably doesn't want to be thanked? A handwritten card feels too stiff, too formal. A batch of cookies is too easy. Then, while turning a corner in my mind, my eyes catch on the wicker basket I brought home from the secondhand shop earlier this week. It's sitting by the door, a little lopsided but still sturdy, its handle smooth with age.

An idea sparks.

A picnic.

The word flits through me like a butterfly. Not a date—not exactly—but a thank-you. A way to show him I see what he did, that I appreciate it. I picture us sitting out by the fields, maybe not the prettiest ones, maybe still tangled with weeds. Flowers nodding in the breeze. Sandwiches wrapped in parchment. Lemonade in mason jars.

The image makes me happy in a way I haven't felt in a long time.

I laugh at myself as I pick up the basket, twirling it by the handle.

"What am I doing?" I mutter.

But the answer is obvious—I'm saying thank you, Hazel-style. Which apparently involves baskets and fields and a whole lot of hope that Beau Rosewood will show up without running in the opposite direction.

I set the basket on the counter, already mentally ticking off what I'll need: bread, cheese, maybe some fruit from the market. Flowers, of course—there has to be a bouquet. I'll make it simple, just like the stand, and pray it doesn't feel silly.

Even if he hates every second, even if he grumbles and critiques my choices the whole time, I'll know I tried. I'll know I didn't let gratitude sit unspoken.

The farmers market is already bustling when I pull into the square, every corner alive with color and chatter. The scent of baked bread mixes with fresh herbs and the faint tang of kettle corn, and for a second, I just stand there in the middle of it all, my basket looped over my arm, trying not to look like a tourist.

My eyes dart from booth to booth—bright vegetables stacked in neat pyramids, jars of golden honey that shimmer when they're moved, bouquets of sunflowers and wild greenery spilling from galvanized tubs. And suddenly I see it.

A vision.

A Pine & Petal stall, right here. Rows of mason jars brimming with marigolds, lavender tied up in little bundles, a chalkboard with hand-lettered prices, maybe even sachets of dried petals tucked into baskets. I imagine chatting with customers, kids tugging at their parents' hands, someone asking if I could make a custom bouquet for an anniversary dinner.

My heart pounds, not from nerves but from the raw possibility of it all. This could be more than a roadside stand. This could be a whole future.

Then I catch myself.

"Nope," I mutter, shaking my head, gripping the handle of my basket tighter. "Not today."

Because this trip is not about potential. It's not about spreadsheets or business plans or what-if scenarios that spin my brain into a frenzy. This trip is about Beau. About thanking him in a way that feels more me than anything else.

I head for the bread stall and lift a crusty loaf, its warmth pressing pleasantly against my hands. At the cheese booth, I linger too long over wedges and samples before finally choosing a creamy brie wrapped neatly in wax paper. I tuck in a jar of strawberry preserves, some apples, and a little bundle of shortbread cookies because—well, cookies.

The basket is starting to look less like groceries and more like a plan. Grinning at myself, I am pleased with my haul.

"Operation Picnic of Gratitude," I whisper, though the name feels clunky. I try again. "Project Thank-a-Beau?" That one makes me snort out loud, earning a look from the vendor across the aisle. I duck my head, laughing into my shoulder.

It's ridiculous, this whole idea. But it's so me. And as I slip a small bunch of sunflowers into the basket—because of course flowers belong in the thank-you picnic and I don't have *these*—I feel that fizz of excitement again.

Beau

THE LATE-NIGHT TRUCE

I drop the shears on the workbench, rub the ache out of my wrists, and tell myself I'm done for the day.

That's when I see her. Hazel.

She's coming up the orchard path, a wicker basket hanging from her arm like she just stepped out of some painting. Her hair's a little wild, cheeks pink from the walk, and for reasons I'd rather not name, my body stiffens.

I school my face into something neutral. "You lost?"

She rolls her eyes, and damn if it doesn't make me want to smile. "Hardly. I came for you."

"That so?" I cross my arms, hiding the way my joints protest.

"Yes." Hazel nods, shifting the basket higher on her arm. "And before you say no, hear me out."

I arch a brow. "You already sound like trouble."

"Probably," she admits, a grin tugging at her mouth. "But I was hoping you'd join me . . . for a picnic. Just to say thank you—for helping, for spreading the word about the flower stand."

My throat works. She knows? Damn Gideon's grandson and his big mouth.

"I didn't—" I start.

"You did. And I appreciate it." She cuts me off with a look

For a long beat, I don't answer. My head screams no. But the way she's standing there, stubborn and soft all at once, makes me want to say yes. Against every ounce of better judgment, I mutter, "Fine. But only because you'd probably camp out here until I agreed."

Her laugh is brighter than the afternoon sun. "Maybe."

She holds on to the basket, and I refrain from making a joke about her strength to carry it herself.

The basket looks ridiculous in her hands—like something a kid would carry to a storybook meadow. But Hazel doesn't seem to notice. Or maybe she does, and she just doesn't care.

She spreads the blanket in the field anyway. The flowers aren't much to look at yet—patchy rows, gaps where blooms haven't come in—but she acts like it's a palace garden.

I lower myself down with more stiffness than I'd like to admit, trying not to wince. Hazel unpacks bread wrapped in linen, little jars of jam, and wedges of cheese. All thrifted-chic and mismatched, but damn if it doesn't look better than anything I've had in weeks.

"This is your thank-you?" I ask, more gruff than I mean to sound.

"Yes." She hands me a slice of bread, smiling like it's the best bargain she's ever struck. "Unless you'd prefer a handwritten note and a pat on the back."

I snort. "Guess this'll do."

For a while, we eat in easy silence. The kind where her knee brushes mine and I don't move away. The kind where I catch myself listening to her hum instead of the cicadas.

She talks about the market, about ideas she has for a booth—chalkboard signs, little bundles of flowers tied with twine. She gets herself worked up, I can see it, her brain sprinting ahead of her hands.

"Careful," I say, breaking a piece of cheese. "You'll burn yourself out before you've even set up the thing."

Hazel pauses, then exhales like she knows I'm right. "I do that sometimes."

"Sometimes?" I arch a brow.

Her laugh bubbles out, soft and self-deprecating. "Okay, a lot."

Warmth rises in me, catching me off guard. It feels easy. Dangerous.

I shift, and the movement sends a sharp ache up my wrist. My grip falters, the bread nearly slipping. Hazel notices. Of course she does.

"You alright?" she asks, voice low.

I nod too fast. "Just sore. Comes with the job."

"From the orchard?"

"From life," I mutter, then regret it when her brow creases.

She doesn't press, though. Just waits, her eyes steady on me.

"Some days it's like my body's older than it should be. Stiff. Slow. Like I can't quite keep up with myself anymore."

"That must be hard." Her face softens in a way I don't deserve.

"You get used to it."

But the lie tastes bitter. I don't get used to it. I just learn to hide it.

Hazel moves closer, so close I can see flecks of gold in her eyes. She doesn't pity me. She just sees me. And that's worse, somehow.

I should say something else. Redirect. Put distance back between us. But then she tilts her chin, just a little, like she's daring me.

And I'm lost.

I kiss her. Soft at first, cautious, like testing a boundary I'm sure will give way. Her lips are warm, tasting faintly of strawberry jam, and when she makes the quietest sound in the back of her throat, I'm gone.

Damn her.

Damn how easy this feels.

Damn how good she tastes.

My hand lifts before I can stop it, thumb brushing her cheek, fingers tangling in the loose strands of her hair. She leans in, answering me with a boldness that makes me ache worse than my condition ever could.

The world fades—the flowers, the aching joints, the years I've spent keeping everyone at arm's length. It's just her.

I almost say it. Almost admit how dangerous this is, how badly I want more. But the words burn in my throat, and I can't let them free. Not yet.

I pull back instead, breathing hard, feeling like I've stepped into something I can't undo.

Hazel's smile is small, steady. Not demanding, not pushing. Just there.

"Thank you, Beau," she whispers, and I know she means more than just the kiss.

Hazel

WINNIE-YOU PIG!

My body feels heavy, sluggish, like I've been wrapped in the kind of sleep that takes more than it gives.

I groan, rubbing at my face as I push myself upright. My hair is a tangled mess, my limbs sore.

Coffee. I *need* coffee.

Dragging myself out of bed, I shuffle toward the kitchen, still half-asleep as I go through the motions—grinding beans, filling the pot, pressing the button that will bring me salvation. The scent of dark roast fills the space, and I rest against the counter, rubbing the stiffness from my neck as I wait.

It's only when I take my first sip that something catches my eye outside—and immediately I choke.

A massive, dirt-covered pig stands right in the middle of my backyard, its snout buried in the remains of last night's picnic. Cheese, crumbs, and an entire piece of forgotten bread are being devoured like a five-star meal.

"Oh my God." My voice comes out strangled.

The pig doesn't care. It keeps eating, its tail giving a lazy flick.

Panic surges through me. What am I supposed to do? Are there wild pigs in Maple Hollow? Did I accidentally summon this beast by leaving food out? What if it charges me? Do pigs charge people?

My phone is in my hand before I realize what I'm doing. I don't even think, I just hit call.

"Hello?" my mom answers, groggily.

"*Mom*," I whisper-yell, pressing my forehead to the glass. "There's a *pig* in my yard."

A pause. "What?"

"A pig," I hiss. "A real one. Huge. It's eating my picnic leftovers."

There's a long silence, then, "Honey, why are you calling me about this?"

"Because I don't know what to do!"

I hear my mom make a small sound, a sigh maybe, like this is just another one of my antics. "I don't know, call animal control? Shoo it away?"

I stare at the pig. It is absolutely *not* the kind of thing you just *shoo* away. It looks like it weighs at least two hundred pounds, and it has tusks. *Tusks*.

"I can't shoo it," I whisper, horrified. "It could kill me."

"Oh, for heaven's sake, Hazel—"

"I am under attack," I insist. "I—oh God, it's looking at me. Mom, it's looking at me."

A low, snorting sound rumbles from the pig's throat, and I swear it's assessing me, deciding whether I am a threat or its next victim.

"Okay, I gotta go," I say, hurriedly. "If I die, tell Maple Hollow I tried."

Before my mom can respond, I hang up, staring at the pig with my heart pounding.

And then, as if the universe heard my silent plea for help, a deep, familiar voice calls out from the other side of the yard.

"You've got to be kidding me."

I whip my head toward the sound—Beau. Standing at the

fence, arms crossed, looking at me like I've somehow personally summoned this pig to ruin his morning.

"Beau," I breathe, relief washing over me. "Help."

He stares at me, a grin forming.

"Beau, please, *help me*," I beg.

Beau rubs a hand down his face. "I was *just* on my way to clean up this mess before this happened. I realize we both were exhausted,"

"*Before this happened?*" I whip around to glare at him. "There is a *beast* in my yard, eating *my* bread, and you're telling me you *knew* this could happen?"

"It's not a beast. It's just old Harold's pig, Winnie. She got loose last week. Damn thing's been terrorizing most of the town, eating whatever it can find."

The pig grunts like it agrees.

I step back as it sniffs the air and takes a slow, lumbering step toward me.

"Beau," I whisper, my voice shaking.

His lips twitch, like he's holding back a laugh. "What, you think it's gonna eat you?"

"I don't know what it's capable of!" I yelp, clutching my coffee like it's a weapon. "It has *tusks!*"

Before he can respond, the pig—Winnie—*charges*.

I scream. Loud. Ear-piercing. The kind of scream that would make any horror movie director proud.

Beau startles, but before he can do anything, something inside me *snaps*. Adrenaline surges through my veins, hot and wild. My body moves before my brain can stop it. I *run* straight at the pig.

"*Get the hell away from my memories!*" I roar at the top of my lungs, arms flailing like a banshee.

The pig skids to a stop, seemingly just as confused as Beau, who looks at me like I've completely lost it.

"Hazel, what the *hell*—"

But I don't stop. I chase after the pig, kicking dirt,

screaming nonsense, fueled by something deep and raw inside me.

"Bad Winnie, *go home now!*" I growl, pointing my finger at the pig as if parenting the large thing.

Winnie lets out a startled squeal before turning on their hooves and *bolting* toward the fence, squeezing through a gap and disappearing into the orchard.

Silence.

I stand there, panting, dirt on my knees, coffee splattered on my shirt. Beau stares at me, completely dumbfounded. I let out a short, breathless laugh. Then another. And then I crumple onto the porch steps, head in my hands.

"This is a memory," I say softly, more to myself than to him. Looking over the remnants of what is left of last night. I take a shuddering breath. "This is a memory, I want to keep . . ."

Beau doesn't say anything for a long moment. Then, finally, he steps closer, lowering himself onto the porch next to me.

His voice is quiet. "What kind of memory?"

I swallow hard, blinking at the ground, but I don't answer. Not yet. I don't feel like I have to.

I sit there for a while, the adrenaline slowly ebbing from my body, leaving me both exhausted and somehow lighter. Beau stays silent beside me, his presence steady, but he doesn't push me for answers. He doesn't need to.

Eventually, I stand up, brushing the dirt off myself, the cool morning air hitting my skin like a reminder of reality. I can hear the faint rustling of the orchard in the distance.

"Thanks for . . . well, thanks," I mumble, more to fill the awkward silence than anything else.

Beau nods but says nothing. It's clear he's still processing my meltdown. He gives a half-grin, like he's not sure whether to laugh or keep his distance. "You're welcome, I guess."

He walks back toward the orchard for a moment, then turns away.

I had plans for big things today, but now? I wanted to hide in bed.

～

The next morning, I wake up with that same restless tug. Instead of scrolling or lingering in bed, I head straight for the kitchen table, arms full of seed packets I've been collecting. I see a plan forming as I spread them out like puzzle pieces.

I drag my laptop closer and pull up a blank spreadsheet.

By afternoon, I'm thumbing through the stack of books Lody sold me, dog-earing pages, and scribbling notes in the margins. Succession planting. Companion flowers. Pest control without chemicals. My handwriting fills the edges like I'm mapping a future I haven't dared before.

Out back, I clear space beside the shed and wrestle together the greenhouse kit I ordered. The frame rattles, the panels resist, but eventually it clicks into place, a crooked little box of potential. Inside, the air is already warmer, almost humming with promise.

When I step back with dirt smudges streaking my arms, I feel it—that rhythm I've been craving. The part of me that once tracked analytics and projections is now charting bloom cycles and watering schedules. Order and chaos, *finally* working together.

Beau

"IT'S GOOD WORK."

The shears don't want to cooperate with me today. My grip slips, the cut comes rough. The branch splinters where it should've been clean. I bite back a curse, jaw tight as I reposition the tool. The joint in my thumb flares, hot and stiff, refusing to move the way I need it to. I stop, flex my fingers, then immediately regret it when pain bites down deeper.

I'm used to this—working through it, forcing my body to bend to the will of the orchard. But some days it feels like the orchard knows I'm faltering. Like the trees can sense weakness and test me with it.

I line up another branch, but my hand trembles at the hinge of the shears. The cut comes jagged again, wasteful, and frustration churns. I drop the branch into the pile at my feet, press the heel of my hand against my thigh, and exhale through clenched teeth.

"Need a hand?"

Her voice slices through the quiet like a bell, sharp enough that I jolt and look over my shoulder. Hazel's standing behind the fence post, half in shadow, like she's been there long enough to see me fail. She pushes away from the post and walks closer, her boots crunching over the frost-hardened ground.

"I can handle it," I say quickly. Too quickly. My tone comes out harder than I meant, rough around the edges.

Hazel doesn't flinch. Her gaze dips to the stack of crooked branches, then to the pruning shears clenched in my fist. "Looks like the trees are winning."

I bristle, straightening my shoulders. "They're not winning. Just takes time to do it right."

She doesn't argue. Doesn't push. Instead, she reaches for the roll of twine dangling from my belt. My instinct is to pull it away, guard it, keep it mine, but she takes it slow, almost asking without words. "I can tie while you cut. Might make the work go faster."

"Not necessary."

"Doesn't mean it wouldn't help," she says, looping the twine loosely in her hands. Her voice is light, but her eyes—steady, calm—are serious. "You do the cutting. I'll tie the branches back so they don't sag. That way we don't waste what's already grown."

Something prickles in me. Not pity. Not concern disguised as kindness. Just practicality. Like she sees this not as charity, but as normal teamwork. That unsettles me more than pity would have.

I hesitate long enough for her to step closer, waiting me out. Finally, I let out a breath and nod once. "Fine."

Her smile is quick, not smug, just satisfied that I let her in. She crouches by the first tree, fingers moving as she threads the twine around a low-hanging branch. Her knot isn't pretty, but it holds. Strong. I move beside her, cutting where the limbs tangle or choke out new growth.

We find a rhythm, and against my better judgment, it feels natural. She doesn't ask if I'm in pain. Doesn't make small talk about the weather to fill the silence. She just hums under her breath, some tune I don't know, and ties her knots while I prune. The quiet between us doesn't press or demand—it just settles, like it belongs here.

By the fourth tree, the tension in my chest is worse than the ache in my hands. I don't know how to handle the sight of her working alongside me, sleeves rolled up, hair falling into her face as she gets close to the bark. I don't know how to handle the way she doesn't treat me like I'm fragile.

When we finish the row, she stands and stretches, brushing dirt from her jeans.

"See?" she says, nodding at the straighter branches, the neater cuts. "Cleaner. Faster."

"Cleaner, maybe," I grunt, setting the shears on my hip.

She tilts her head, studying me like she can see past the words I won't say. Then she smiles, small but sure. "It's good work, Beau."

The words land heavier than they should. I force my eyes away, focusing on the orchard beyond us. Rows of trees stretching out, silent witnesses to a truth I don't want spoken aloud—I didn't do this alone.

I mutter something about needing to sharpen the shears, but my throat is thick, the words heavy. Because part of me wants to thank her, admit how much easier it was with her there. Another part—the louder part—wants to build the wall back up, to shove her help into the corner with everything else I refuse to need.

But she doesn't wait for me to sort it out. She just pats the dirt off her hands, slings the twine back over the fence post, and says, "I'll see you around."

And then she's gone, her boots carrying her back toward her side of the field, leaving behind the faint trace of lavender and sweat and something I can't name.

I stand there longer than I should, the shears heavy in my hand. The pain in my fingers is sharp, but it's not what unsettles me most.

What unsettles me is her acceptance. The way she worked

beside me was like it was the most natural thing in the world. The way she didn't look at me like I was broken.

And I don't know what to do with that.

And like a fool, my mind slips backward, uninvited, to the other night.

That kiss.

I can still feel it if I let myself. The soft press of her mouth against mine, warm and tentative at first, then—God help me—sure, like she meant it. I remember the way her hand had lingered against me, steadying herself or maybe steadying me, I don't know.

All I know is the taste of her, the heat, the way the world narrowed to nothing but her breath and her pulse against me.

It isn't supposed to be that easy. It isn't supposed to feel that good.

I tighten my grip on the shears until my knuckles throb, forcing myself back into the present. Back to the orchard. Back to the ache in my hands that I understand better than the ache she's left behind.

I tell myself it was just a kiss. A thank-you wrapped in impulse. Nothing more.

But when I close my eyes, I see her looking at me like she knows something I don't want to admit.

And I can't stop thinking about how badly I want to taste her again.

Hazel

PLEASE

"*See you around*"? Really? I kiss the man and then dismiss him like we're two strangers passing on the street. Smooth, Hazel. Real smooth.

Since then, I've been tiptoeing around Beau like he's a patch of wet paint I don't dare smudge. I catch glimpses of him in the orchard or hauling crates near the barn, and every time, my heart does that ridiculous stutter-step, like I'm back in middle school with my very first crush. I'm a grown woman with a failed career and dirt under her fingernails, and yet—he smiles at me, and suddenly I'm a schoolgirl again.

The day slips away fast—seed trays, greenhouse chores, checking the soil moisture—and before I know it, the sky is blushing toward evening. My stomach reminds me I haven't eaten since breakfast, so I wander down to the diner.

Inside, the air hums with chatter and the smell of fried onions. Maggie is in full force behind the counter, her voice carrying clear across the room.

"Sterling tea, all the way from Havenwood!" she crows, holding up a tin like it's a treasure chest. "Ophelia brought it herself, bless her heart. You can taste the sunshine in every leaf."

I can't even begin to unpack whatever story she's weaving, so I tune her out—because Beau is here. He's tucked into his usual corner booth, broad shoulders hunched, a plate half-finished in front of him.

And then I do the stupidest thing. I slide into his booth. Not across from him, like a normal human being. No—I make myself right at home next to him, close enough to catch his faint, woodsy smell, close enough to feel the bench shift under his weight.

His fork pauses midair.

"Hazel." His voice is quiet, careful.

"Hi." My smile feels wobbly. "Mind if I—uh—sit?"

"You already did." There's a twitch at the corner of his mouth, like he can't decide if he's amused or confused.

"Right." I fold my hands on the table, staring at the salt shaker like it holds the secrets of the universe. My pulse hammers in my throat, but I force myself to push forward. If I don't say this now, I'll never say it.

"So . . . I've been thinking," I start, my voice low, so only he can hear. "About the farm. About what it could be . . . I want to host a late-summer flower market," I say in a rush. "Something open to the community. Bouquets, wreaths, maybe even some workshops. Music, food trucks, if I can swing it. A day where people can come out, walk the fields, and take a little piece of it home."

There. Out in the air between us.

Beau blinks, slow and skeptical. "A flower market."

"Yes." My cheeks burn, but I don't back down. "On the farm. By the end of the season."

"Hazel, that's . . . ambitious." He rests against the booth, arms crossed. "You've barely got things off the ground. Do you really think you can pull something like that together?"

The words sting. "I know it sounds crazy. But I want to try. I don't want this place to just survive—I want it to bloom.

And maybe that means doing things before they feel safe. Before they feel certain."

His gaze lingers on me, like he's searching for cracks, for the part where I'll admit defeat and laugh it off. But I don't. I hold his eyes, steady as I can.

"This is about hope," I say softly. "I'm choosing hope. Even if no one else does."

The silence stretches. Then Beau exhales, long and heavy, his shoulders softening just a fraction. I am waiting for words to escape his mouth.

But Beau doesn't answer right away. He just sits there, fork forgotten, arms crossed like a shield. I can *see* him trying to be his gruff, practical self—the part of him that leans on caution, that says no before yes. His jaw is set, his eyes narrow like he's bracing himself against the storm I just invited into the booth.

But then, for just a heartbeat, he softens. His shoulders ease, his eyes flicker down to the table like he's letting himself imagine it—my dream, the market, the laughter and color and life spilling out over this tired land.

It vanishes just as quickly. The wall snaps back into place. His mouth goes tight again. He appears every bit the skeptical orchard man who doesn't have time for pie-in-the-sky dreams.

And then—he looks at me. Not just *at me*, but *at my mouth*. The kind of look that makes my skin prickle and my pulse stumble. Like he might kiss me again, right here in Maggie's diner, with the scent of fried onions hanging in the air and the hum of other people's conversations surrounding us. Like he might devour me whole if I let him.

I swallow hard because the heat that floods me is almost too much. I don't know why I do it—maybe because his silence is unbearable, maybe because my heart is too loud—but I slip my hand onto his thigh under the table. His muscles tense under my palm.

"Please believe in me," I whisper, the words tumbling out before I can stop them. It doesn't make sense—I know his approval isn't the key to any of this. My choices are mine. My dream is mine. But still, in some small, silly way, I *need* it. I value it.

Beau doesn't speak. He drops his gaze to where my hand rests on him, his lashes shadowing his eyes. Then slowly, he lays his calloused hand over mine. Heavy, steady. A touch that says more than words could.

He doesn't say it. But I know. Somehow, deep down, I know he already does.

The moment is short.

"Can I take your order?" Saffron's voice is light, practiced, but her eyes dip—not at my face, not at Beau's, but to our joined hands under the table. Then she flicks her gaze back up at Beau, as if waiting for him to move, to brush me off.

He doesn't. Instead, his hand presses harder over mine, his grip tightening in quiet defiance, like he wants her to see. To know.

Heat races up my neck. I clear my throat. "Uh—coffee. Black, please. And a slice of the apple crumble, if you've got it."

Saffron jots it down, but I catch the little trinket clipped to her lanyard—a round pin with a mountain etched against a dusky sky. The Cascades, unmistakable.

I can't stop the lift that comes over me. "You're from the Pacific Northwest?"

Her face brightens, breaking into a grin. "Yeah, born and raised. A little town just east of Seattle. My dad still runs a coffee shop there."

The words tumble out of her, warm and alive, and it is like I've been starved for a piece of home I didn't even realize I missed. I ask the name of the shop, how long it's been around, what it smells like when you walk in. Saffron laughs softly, describing the scent of espresso that seeps into the floorboards and the way her dad still insists on roasting his own beans.

I drink in every word. It feels like standing in the drizzle again, pine trees stretching high above, the hum of coffee shops on every corner. I didn't know how much I missed it until now.

But even as I'm caught in her stories, I feel him. Beau. Watching me. Not my hands this time, not my eyes. My mouth. Again. Like every word that slips past my lips is something he wants to claim for himself. A silent heat makes my heart pound louder than it should for a simple conversation about coffee.

I try not to look at him. I know if I do, I'll see the truth of it in his eyes.

But then I do it. I glance over, reckless, and catch him in the act.

Beau isn't just studying me. He's fighting with himself.

His teeth clenched, his shoulders wound up like he's bracing against a storm only he can feel. But it's his eyes that undo me—dark, tired, carrying years of weight I can't even name. And beneath all of that, something raw and unguarded. A man begging himself not to want. A man who's been convincing himself for so long that wanting is weakness.

Except right now, he's losing that battle.

I see it—hunger, hesitation, exhaustion, and longing—tangled up in one man, in one look that pierces straight through me.

My breath catches, because it's not just attraction, not just a crush. This is deeper, older somehow, like roots tangling before I even knew they were growing.

And it changes me. It changes *everything*. Like someone reached inside and rewired my whole brain, like every thought will now be colored by this moment—by him.

Beau mutters something about needing air, sliding out of the booth, and before I can think twice, I'm on my feet too. The diner's warm chatter fades as I trail him into the night, the cool air biting against my flushed skin.

He doesn't waste a second. The moment we're near his

truck, he turns, his hand catching my wrist like it's the most natural thing in the world. In a heartbeat, he pulls me inside the dark cab, and the world muffles.

I barely have time to breathe before he hauls me onto his lap. My knees hit the worn seat, his hands anchor my hips, and I can feel the solid heat of him beneath me.

"Beau—" My voice is shaky, uncertain, but threaded with something that betrays me.

Want.

His breath fans hot against my cheek, ragged, like he's been holding this in far too long. He's all rough edges, all gruff restraint that's unraveling under my touch, under *me*.

He pulls back just far enough to drag his gaze over me—like he's memorizing every line, every inch—and I swear my body hums under the weight of it.

"Damn you," he whispers, voice hoarse.

I tilt my head, meeting his eyes, letting the corner of my mouth curve in something bolder than I feel. "You're the one who pulled me out here."

The muscle in his jaw flexes, like he wants to argue, but he doesn't. He can't.

Something inside me snaps loose, sultry and sure in a way that shocks even me. I lean closer, let my lips brush the shell of his ear, my voice a low whisper. "Please."

That one word wrecks him.

A sound escapes him—half moan, half surrender—as I settle my full weight down, pressing us together in a way that leaves no space for denial. His hands clutch harder at my waist, his restraint breaking, and I see it. I feel it. The exact moment Beau Rosewood stops fighting himself and gives in completely.

"Say it again," he says, hot against my neck, his voice all gravel and need.

My breath catches, my fingers fisting in the fabric of his shirt like I might float away if I don't anchor myself. My lips brush his ear, and I whisper, shaky but certain, "P-please, Beau."

He shudders beneath me, a sound tearing from his chest that's equal parts hunger and surrender. His forehead drops against my shoulder, his grip on my waist tightening as if he can't bear to let go. For a heartbeat, the whole world feels like it's just this truck cab, just his rough breaths and my pounding pulse.

Then, slowly, he pulls back, his eyes catching mine in the dark. There's fire there, but also something deeper, something that terrifies me even as it makes me ache. Neither of us moves, neither of us speaks. We just stay there, suspended, everything unsaid thick in the air between us.

And I know—this is only the beginning.

Beau

BLOOMING ADMIRATION

It's been a few days, and I've been catching myself in better moods than usual. Not big, obvious smiles—just little things. Like when the coffee maker didn't sputter for once. Or when the orchard cat decided to drop a dead mouse on the porch instead of in my boots. Even found myself chuckling when the rooster crowed late, like he'd forgotten his job.

Might be nothing. Or—it might be the other night in the truck, Hazel saying my name like she meant it.

I don't let myself linger on that thought too long. Best not to.

What I can't ignore is Hazel herself. She's been busy. Out in front of the farmhouse, painting signs, her hair tied up, messy and streaked with pale blue paint. Lining mason jars across her porch rail, each one holding test bouquets. Sometimes she frowns at them like they've failed a test, sometimes she beams like she's cracked a secret code.

And when she's not fussing with flowers, she's got papers spread out across the picnic table—charts, notes, things I don't even bother trying to understand. She looks at them the way I look at orchard ledgers, brow furrowed, lips pressed tight. Serious. Determined.

It stirs up something I haven't thought about in years—my folks' first harvest festival. I was a kid, maybe ten, sticky with candied apple, running under string lights while Pa sold cider by the gallon. Neighbors brought pies, kids lined up to show off prize pumpkins. Folks laughed, argued, ate too much. The whole town breathing together like it mattered

Hazel reminds me of that. Her stubborn little flower stand, her paint-streaked signs, her charts—she's trying to build something that could pull people together again.

And I'll be damned if I don't want her to succeed. Not just for her. For Maple Hollow.

Even if hope's a dangerous thing for a man like me, I can't quite keep it out anymore. Not when she's out there humming to herself, like she already knows it'll all work out.

The thought is still settling when my phone buzzes in my pocket. I tug off a glove with my teeth, swiping to answer. "Yeah?"

"Beau," Maggie's voice comes sharp and frazzled. "You busy?"

I eyes find Hazel bent over her jars in the distance. My thumb rubs absently over the handle of my shears. "Always. Why?"

"Pipe burst under the diner sink. Floodin' fast. I called the plumber, but he's out on another job. I need someone who can shut it off before my whole kitchen floats away."

"I'll be there in ten."

"Make it five," she snaps and hangs up.

I groan, but pocket the phone. Another glance toward Hazel, and then I grab my truck keys.

Work never stops in Maple Hollow. Neither does she.

I pull the truck up to the diner, gravel crunching under the tires. The place smells like frying bacon and coffee, even from the lot. Maggie's waving me in from the door, hands on her hips, a perfect blend of exasperation and relief that only comes with small-town life.

"Glad you made it," she says, voice pitched somewhere between irritation and gratitude. "I've got water everywhere, and the mop's about as useful as a screen door on a submarine."

"Where's the culprit?" I slide out of the truck, boots scuffing against the gravel.

"Under the sink. Apparently, it wanted to explore my kitchen. You better hope your hands are steadier than mine, Rosewood."

I kneel, ignoring the pain, twist the valves, and a gush of water sputters before finally obeying. Maggie watches, arms crossed, tapping her foot impatiently. "You always this heroic, Beau, or just when the world needs a miracle in my kitchen?"

"Only on Tuesdays," I mutter, tightening the final connection. "And today happens to be Tuesday."

"Figures." Maggie laughs, shaking her head. "Can't do anything simple, can you?"

I let my gaze wander out the window just long enough for Hazel's figure to flash in my mind. She'd be out there in the sun, dirt smudges and paint on her hands, plotting something new for her flower stand. For a second, I almost want to sneak off and see what she's doing—but I can't. Not yet.

"Beau?" Maggie nudges my shoulder. "You awake in there? Everything good?"

"Yeah," I say, snapping back. "All fixed. Shouldn't flood again unless the universe really hates you."

"Don't spend it all at once," she jokes, slipping me a bag of peanut butter cookies as payment. "How's the neighbor? Busy?"

My insides tighten, and I force my gaze back toward the sink. "Yeah. She's . . . busy."

"Busy, huh?" Maggie teases. "Better keep an eye on that one. Folks in town are already talking about her little flower stand."

I nod. Hazel is chasing her dream. And Maple Hollow is getting a taste of her energy.

"Thanks, dear. Really."

"Alright, I'm done here. Keep the diner standing while I go check on my orchard before the day's lost."

Maggie waves me off, shaking her head with a smile. "You and your hero complexes."

I don't answer. I just walk back toward the truck, feeling that tug, that little ache that comes with wanting someone else's world to flourish. Hazel's world. And the funny, dangerous thing is—I'm not sure I even want it to flourish without me in it.

Hazel

REROUTE

I drag myself across the field, shoulders slumped, arms heavy with nothing but disappointment. The air is harsh and unforgiving, baking my back, and I stop mid-step, letting it press down like a weight I can't shrug off. I stare at the flower beds—the ones I've been tending for weeks—barely a whisper of color left.

A lump forms in my throat, and then it bursts. I sink to my knees, heaving, hands trembling. Tears burn my eyes and slide down my cheeks, smearing dirt into streaks that make me look caught between rage and defeat. Every plan I made, every spreadsheet, every PinBoard, every late-night sketch—it all feels meaningless. This farm, these blooms, my home-market dream . . . It feels undoable, I have enough for some arrangements, but not on a P&P Market level.

I sob, the sound coming out in ragged gasps, and I can't stop. My body shakes with frustration, grief, and an aching, stubborn sort of hope that's screaming to survive even as I collapse under it. I feel like an infant, like a child throwing a tantrum because life didn't go her way. And maybe, right now, that's exactly what I am.

I stumble toward Beau's house, dragging my self-conscious, messy body across the grass. My robe flaps around my knees, the fabric damp with sweat and tears. I climb onto his porch swing without thinking, letting my entire self slump into the chains, my feet dragging against the planks. I can't hide the pout, the mess, the ache, the humiliation—I'm just too broken for it.

Beau's boots crunch across the gravel behind me, careful, steady. He doesn't say anything at first. And then, soft but firm, he speaks.

"You're going to figure this out."

I blink through my tears, sniffle, and shift slightly, just enough to catch his eyes. They're calm, but not cold—steady, certain, like he knows something I don't yet.

"You're tougher than these mountains," he continues, and I can hear the weight of every word. "Tougher than the things life throws at you. Tougher than life itself."

I stare at him, mouth open a little. His certainty presses into me like a lighthouse beam, cutting through the storm in my mind. For a heartbeat, I feel something steady anchor inside me—a pulse of possibility, quiet but insistently bright.

"You know why I'm so grumpy?" he says finally, voice low, almost rough.

I tilt my head, studying him, letting the question hang there. "No," I admit softly. "I don't."

He lets out a dry laugh, not a cheerful one, more like the kind that holds years of frustration. "Because there's a lot I can't do anymore. Stuff I should've been able to do, stuff I wanted to do. Pain keeps me in check whether I like it or not."

He's opening a door I didn't know was there, and I can't help moving a little closer. "I . . . I didn't realize."

"Rheumatoid arthritis," he says, almost matter-of-factly, like he's talking about the weather. "My joints fight me every damn day. Some days, I can't even grip a hammer without it screaming at me." He flexes his hands slowly, the tendons stiff, the knuckles swollen. "And there's no taking a day off, no quitting, no rest that really helps. You adapt. Or you break."

My heart twists at the vulnerability he rarely lets anyone see. He runs a hand through his hair and peers out toward the flower fields.

"When the Marshalls sold the place . . . it was like someone ripped a piece of my childhood right out from under me. My Pa, he loved flowers, but he kept the orchard alive in honor of his own Pa. Every tree, every bloom had a memory tucked into it. When the Marshalls just handed it off, I . . . it broke me a little."

"Because your dad wasn't here to buy it?" I whisper.

"Yeah." He nods, staring at the darkened rows of apple trees. "Even though I could've—technically, legally, financially—I couldn't. My hands wouldn't let me. My body wouldn't let me. So I saw three different families move in and out, none of them even unpacking properly, none of them caring about it the way it deserved. But you . . ." He turns toward me, eyes narrowing just enough to soften instead of glare. "You unpacked. You rooted yourself. In these mountains. In the soil. In my . . . In my heart. And hell, you're still standing here, all stubborn, all alive, even if you can't drink the well water without wincing."

I blink, caught off guard. My hands rest in my lap, trembling a little from the intensity of it all. "I . . . I just wanted to be here. To try. To belong."

His heart.

He lets out a growl, shaking his head. "You belong. You belong more than anyone who came before. And it's not just because of the farm or the flowers or whatever this crazy little dream of yours is. It's you. You're one tough woman, Hazel. And hell, I might be grumpy, but I notice."

"I don't know if I can live up to that." I laugh softly, shakily, the sound trembling through me.

"You already are." Beau shrugs, the movement casual but

deliberate. "You just don't always see it." He pauses, then smirks—a gruffness softened by warmth, that impossible combination that makes me ache—a sweet ache.

He bends closer, voice lowering, intimate without words, almost conspiratorial.

"You can still have your dream," he says. "Just . . . on a smaller scale."

And suddenly, a spark ignites inside me. Not a blaze, not a wildfire—but a steady, sure flame. I can do this. I can make this market happen, even if it's not the massive, lavish dream I first pictured. I can start small. I can test the waters. I can sell at the farmers market. I can survive—and thrive—in baby steps.

I grin, then laugh, a little hysterical, a little incredulous, a little relieved. "The farmers market! Beau, the farmers market! That's perfect! I can do it—That is the smaller scale!"

Beau's chuckle is low and amused. He shakes his head, like he's been roped into my excitement whether he wants to be or not. He follows me inside as I flail toward the house, bouncing on the balls of my feet with reckless enthusiasm, my robe flaring around me.

Inside, I flood the kitchen table with notebooks, sticky notes, seed charts, color swatches, and rough sketches of booth layouts. Beau gazes at me from the counter as I spill my plans across every inch of surface. He doesn't interrupt—doesn't roll his eyes or sigh, like he might with anyone else. He just lets me talk, letting the words tumble out, letting the energy carry him along.

I describe every detail. The booth size, signage, pricing, test bouquets, even the way I want to fold the little ribbon bows. He listens. Really listens. And every now and then, I catch him smiling—just a little, just enough to see that the gruff, quiet man I've come to know is softening around the edges.

Hours slip by unnoticed. We sketch, calculate, debate, and

brainstorm until the lamp's glow is the only light left in the house. My energy ebbs into a happy, giddy exhaustion. Beau's presence is a steady pulse beside me, comforting and real. His hand brushes mine when we reach for the same marker, a casual, unintentional connection that sends a spark straight up my arm.

By two in the morning, my limbs finally demand rest. We collapse onto the couch together, sprawling awkwardly in our fatigue, and I let myself sink against him. His arm wraps around me naturally, protectively, and I press my head against his body. It's warm. Solid. Safe. And it's mine to enjoy without guilt, without shame, without expectation.

I close my eyes, my mind still buzzing with color palettes, bloom schedules, and booth designs. One step. One small, glorious step at a time. And Beau . . . he's still here, steady, quiet, and completely entwined in this new life of mine.

I drift off with the quiet certainty that I *can* do this. I *will* do this. Baby steps first, bloom by bloom. I fall asleep thinking that Beau here beside me makes every one of those steps a little easier.

Beau

A DAY WITH YOU

I rise before the world stirs, muscles protesting from yesterday and last night, but a keen excitement threads through the ache. My phone buzzes on the nightstand. Hazel hasn't stirred yet, probably curled up somewhere in her little nest of blankets and half-used notebooks.

I squint at the screen. Amanda—our event coordinator for the farmers market—just replied. A green light. She's in. My grin spreads like wildfire, and I almost yell out loud, but the room is quiet except for the early hum of the farmhouse. Hazel's going to be thrilled, but I also know she'll try to take on the world all at once if I let her.

When she finally stirs, eyes bleary and hair in every direction except where it belongs, I resist smirking. Almost.

"You got in," I tell her gently, not wanting to startle her.

Her eyes snap open, searching my face, and when it hits her, they light up like a firecracker.

"Wait—what? You—" She sits up too fast and nearly tips off the edge of the bed, flailing like a cartoon. I catch her shoulder just in time. "Beau! Really?"

"Really," I confirm. "You're in. Farmers market, your first big appearance. You're gonna kill it."

Her grin is unstoppable, but I can already see the tension in her shoulders, the way she's itching to run off and do a hundred things at once. I clear my throat, trying to sound as authoritative as I can manage.

"Here's the thing, we need to pace it today. You're exhausted. No matter how many bouquets or spreadsheets or signage ideas you have, we spend the better part of today recouping, or you'll burn yourself out before tomorrow."

Her lips purse, a little pout forming, but she nods. "Okay . . . okay, I'll try."

"Good." I lead the way out, grabbing the keys. "First order of business is breakfast. You're going to need fuel for all that energy of yours."

We pull up at the diner just as the morning light spills across the parking lot. Maggie waves at us from the door, already fussing over food shipments. I ignore her for the moment, letting Hazel's calm take over. She sits, still beaming, and I order us the farmers breakfast platter along with apple crumble because I know she'll cave and share anyway.

The plates come, steaming and fragrant, and we dig in. I take a slow bite, savoring the crisp bacon and eggs, the hash browns perfectly fried. Hazel's eyes sparkle as she tears into the crumble. I notice the faint dark smudges under her eyes, the way she tries to make herself small even though she's anything but.

"So," I start, trying to keep the conversation easy, "only child?"

"Yep." Hazel nods. "I was . . . mostly on my own, really. Dad was traveling constantly, and Mom, well, she was everywhere. Everywhere except around me, but when she was around, it was intense. Helicopter intense. She ran a corporate empire in Seattle, was well respected, and Dad—get this—he is a traveling speaker. Family healing seminars. Ironic, right?" She laughs softly, shaking her head. "I spent a lot of my childhood being ignored by one parent while the other stressed about me being noticed."

I chew slowly, digesting the weight behind her words.

"Yeah, I get the only child thing," I say. "Or at least, the isolation part. I grew up here, orchard and all. Pa and I worked side by side, learned everything together. But it was all expectation, no cushioning, no excuses. Every branch had to be perfect, every row straight. Mistakes weren't allowed. I wasn't allowed." I pause, letting the words settle between us.

"I can see that. I mean, the orchard has always felt like it had rules you can't break, like a silent partner in everything you do."

I shrug, trying to mask the knot in me, the way the old ache in my hands burns even now. "Something like that."

She smiles gently, tilting her head. "I think that's why you get me, Beau. I don't fit the rules either, not exactly. But I'm trying, in my own messy, stubborn way."

"Yeah. I can see that." I can't help the slight grin tugging at my lips.

I stir my coffee slowly, as Hazel pushes a piece of apple crumble around her plate like she's thinking through a complicated puzzle. The diner's morning rush hums softly around us —plates clatter, mugs scrape, the sizzle from the griddle punctuates every so often—but I'm only half aware of it. Most of my focus is on her, on the way her brows furrow when she's deep in thought, the slight tilt of her head as she weighs her words.

"Beau . . ." she says, hesitating, almost a whisper, and I feel her hand hover over her mug. I don't look at her yet, pretending to examine the rim of my plate. I know what's coming. Her tone has that gentle weight—the one that makes me stop whatever mental guard I'm putting up.

"You okay?" she asks softly. Not like Maggie or anyone else would ask.

I catch that spark of vulnerability in her eyes.

"I'm fine," I say. The words sound hollow even to me, but I don't let them see the grit behind them.

She tilts her head toward me. "The other day, when you mentioned . . . your hands. Your joints." Her fingers tap lightly on the table, tracing a rhythm I can't ignore.

"Yes, my rheumatoid arthritis. It flares up. Some days, it's worse than others. Some days, I can barely grip a branch, let alone carry boxes or prune trees. I . . ." I trail off, letting the confession hang.

She doesn't flinch, doesn't recoil. She just nods, quietly, her gaze soft but steady.

"That makes sense," she says gently. "I've seen some days —the way your hands shake—when you're trying not to let it show. Or how you stretch before pruning."

"Most people don't notice." I swallow hard. "And honestly, I like it that way. I've lost enough of my life to it already."

She reaches across the table then, placing her hand lightly over mine. Her touch is warm, grounding, not pitying.

"Beau, it doesn't make you less. If anything, it makes what you do . . . stronger. You've kept this orchard alive, even with it. And now you're helping me. That's remarkable."

I stare at her hand over mine, the subtle pressure saying more than words could.

"You know," she continues, voice low, almost conspiratorial, "I think that's part of why I admire you. You keep going. Even when it hurts. Even when it's inconvenient. Even when it's unfair." She tilts her head, searching my face. "You've had so much taken from you already, Beau, and you still keep giving, still keep trying. I don't know how you do it."

I shrug, trying to make it casual, but I can't hide the pride and the vulnerability wrapped together there. "Some of us have to. Some of us don't have a choice."

She smiles softly, and for a moment the diner fades around us.

Pulling back slightly, her hand leaves mine, but it's still close enough that I can feel her warmth lingering.

"You don't have to talk about it all the time, Beau. Just let me help when I can. That's all I'm asking."

I nod, and the nod feels heavy. Not because I'm agreeing to anything in particular, but because I want to. Want to let her in a little. Want to let someone see what it's like to live inside me without flinching.

She smiles again, lighter this time, and it's enough to make me grin like an idiot. And I let myself stay in that moment a while, her presence filling the space around me in a way I've rarely allowed.

Hazel

FOR REAL THIS TIME

I jolt awake before the alarm, the sun barely peeking over the mountains, the farm is still cloaked in a sleepy haze. My gut coils hard, knotted as tight as pulled rope—I'm supposed to be excited, but all I feel is jittery, a hum of nerves vibrating through my chest. Market day. My first real shot at this, and I keep picturing every possible way it could go wrong.

I shove the covers off and tiptoe to the bathroom, though my nerves make every step feel like a stomp. The shower's hot, almost scalding, but I let it pound into my shoulders, trying to scrub away the anxiety I've been carrying since last night. Steam fills the tiny bathroom, curling around me like a shield, giving me a few moments to breathe, to collect myself. I scrub at my hair until the knots loosen, rinse, and wrap myself in the softest towel I can find.

Getting dressed is another challenge—something professional enough for the public, practical enough for the farm. I settle on the floral dress I wore when I first planned the flower stand, the one that makes me feel capable without being stiff. Comfort and confidence, I tell myself, even if my hands tremble while I button the back.

Packing is worse. Boxes of blooms, the stand sign, ribbons, extra jars, my laptop tucked carefully into its sleeve, the little bag of business cards I made, and a handful of emergency scissors and twine. Beau had been so steady helping me last night, sorting, organizing, making sure I wasn't forgetting anything. I glance at everything and panic anyway, running my hands over each item, double-checking, triple-checking.

Breakfast? I push the thought away. I know if I try to eat, I'll just make the butterflies worse. So I sip water instead, careful not to choke on my own nerves.

I pause, standing in the middle of the living room, looking at all the carefully packed boxes, the tote with the cash box, the small cashless payment device, the fresh flowers still wrapped in damp paper. I breathe in the scent of lavender and marigold and daisies and remember why I wanted this, why I've worked so hard. And then I feel that flutter, that tickle of excitement buried under the fear.

I straighten my shoulders, pick up the first box, and take the first step out the door. Today isn't about perfection. Today isn't about anyone else's approval. Today is about proving to myself that I can do this—even if my stomach threatens mutiny, even if my hands shake, even if my heart beats so fast I'm sure it'll burst.

I take a deep breath of the early morning air, hoist the boxes, and head toward the truck, ready for the first real test of Pine & Petal.

"You ready for this, flower lady?" Beau says, cutting through my anxiety.

I swallow hard and grin, nerves and excitement tangling together. "I think so," I say, though my voice wavers. "Can . . . can you drive? I'd rather not stress myself out trying to navigate."

His brow quirks, showing both amusement and disbelief, and then he opens the door like it's nothing. "Hop in. I've got this."

I climb in, settling into the passenger seat, still gripping the edge of my seat a little. The engine rumbles to life, and I can feel my pulse quicken as we roll down the dusty farm road.

The mountains flank us, the orchard stretching behind us like green-and-gold carpets. I press my hand to the window, observing the fields as they go by, a giddy bubble of happiness rises, ready to burst. Everything feels more real when I see it from this angle, all of Maple Hollow slowly waking up around us.

Beau drives with that calm, steady rhythm. Out of the corner of my eye, his jaw sets, the way his hands grip the wheel. He's focused, but there's a faint light in his eyes—like he's almost smiling just a little because he knows how much this means to me.

The closer we get to town, the faster my heart beats. The little brick-and-wood shops flash past—bookstore, diner, hardware, post office—and I can't stop my eyes from wandering to all the places where my flowers could end up someday. I imagine a row of Pine & Petal bouquets lining the front of the farmers market, and the vision makes me practically vibrate with anticipation.

Beau notices the sparkle in my eyes, and for the first time, I think I see him caught in it too—not the gruff, hard-to-read Beau, but just a man quietly watching someone he cares about get excited about their dreams.

"I can't believe it's finally happening," I whisper, almost to myself.

He chuckles softly. "You've worked hard for this."

"I have," I admit. My breath lifts in a way that has nothing to do with nerves and everything to do with possibility—finally stepping into something I built with my own hands.

And when Beau catches my hand with his, just briefly, I squeeze back.

I hop out of the truck, my arms already aching from the

boxes and bundles I've brought along, but I don't care. This is it—my first day at the market.

Beau slides the last crate down beside me, giving me a half-smile. "You good?"

"I've got this."

The morning breeze is soft but warm, brushing my shoulders as I pull the blankets, ribbons, and jars out of the crate. I start arranging the bouquets, little vases lined up neatly, marigolds, daisies, lavender spilling out in bursts of color. My hands tremble just a little, but I push through.

From behind me, I hear a cheerful voice. "Well, look who finally joined us!"

I turn to see a woman setting up her own booth nearby—her table overflowing with hand-knit scarves and jars of honey. She's smiling warmly, eyes twinkling. "Hazel, right? I've heard about you. Welcome!"

"Oh—thank you," I say, feeling my face heat up. Her enthusiasm is contagious. She reaches over, adjusting a small jar on my table. "Here, let me help with that. You don't want it resting crooked like that. First time?"

I nod, grateful and a little embarrassed. "Yeah . . . first market day."

She laughs, not in a mocking way, but like she remembers that first-time jittery energy. "Don't worry. You're going to be fine. It's a small town. People love a new flower stand. You just get your feet wet, and you'll see."

As I step back, another couple of vendors greet me, shaking my hand, asking about my farm, complimenting the arrangements. One older man with a stall of fresh-baked bread smiles. "If you need a hand moving anything, don't hesitate. We all help each other here."

I feel a little burst of pride, the anxiety slowly loosening its grip.

Beau lingers nearby, hands in his pockets. I can feel his eyes on me, but he doesn't hover or interfere, just keeps me in his peripheral vision. Every so often, our hands brush as I adjust a tablecloth or straighten a vase.

I'm still straightening a bundle of lavender when the first real customer approaches. A woman in a crisp blazer and too-shiny shoes stops in front of my table, hands on her hips. She picks up a mason jar, inspects it, frowns, then squints at the chalkboard sign.

"$12 for . . . that?" she asks, voice sharp, like I've just handed her a bouquet made of weeds. "Do you know how much these cost in the city?"

I open my mouth, but before I can say anything rational, something ridiculous bubbles up out of me—a short, nervous laugh. I cringe immediately.

She blinks, eyebrows raised. "Excuse me?"

I clear my throat, cheeks burning. "I—I know it sounds high, but these flowers are . . . hand-picked. Everything's fresh, and I made the bouquets myself."

She sniffs, sets the jar down a little too firmly, and walks away without another word. A warm, hearty laugh blooms from the booth next to me.

"You alright there, newbie?" It's the honey-and-scarf woman. "I almost spit out my coffee just now. That laugh of yours? Perfect. People need to know you're human, not just some perfect little flower machine."

I blink at her, surprised, relieved, and then laugh again, more genuinely this time.

"Guess I'm human then," I admit, shaking my head. She chuckles with me, giving my shoulder a friendly pat. Beau looks like he was waiting to jump in if that lady kept going.

"Do you have any tips for keeping lavender fresh?" asks an older woman, using her cane to prop herself up. I show her how I trim the stems and change the water daily, and she nods approvingly, offering me a small smile that feels like gold.

Another little boy tugs at his mother's hand and points at the daisies. "Can I pick one?" His mom laughs and says yes, and I hand him a tiny bouquet. He beams as he skips down the aisle.

By the time Beau steps up with a bottle of water, I'm feeling lighter, the nervousness loosening.

"How's it going?" he asks, eyes scanning the booth.

I grin, holding up a bouquet I just finished tying. "Better than I thought it would. People are . . . surprisingly nice, actually."

"See?" He smirks, just a little. "You've got this." Even though it's just those three words, I cling to them.

Throughout the morning, more people stop—neighbors who nod and greet me, other vendors who offer advice or just friendly smiles, a few who linger just to admire the colors. By late morning, I'm laughing, chatting, moving between bouquets and vases with a rhythm I didn't think I had yet.

Somewhere in the middle of it all, I realize I'm no longer just a visitor in this town. I belong, like this market, these flowers, even these first customers, are a part of my life now.

The last bouquet is in my hands—and, just like that, I'm out. Empty table. Nothing is left but the ribbons and vases.

"Looks like it's time to pack up," my vendor neighbor calls over, waving a hand. "Go explore the market. You earned it."

I hesitate, then grin, letting Beau step up beside me. He gives me that small, lopsided smirk I've grown to adore and takes the heavier tote. I sling the rest over my shoulder, feeling weightless in a way I haven't in months.

With the truck all packed, we walk together, arms brushing, then slipping into a subtle entwine. I can feel him relax as we move through the rows of booths—fresh-baked breads, hand-carved wooden spoons, fragrant soaps. He bends slightly toward me, voice low.

"I'm proud of you," he murmurs.

"You really mean that?" I ask, teasing, but with a whisper of hope.

"Mm," he hums, eyes scanning the bustling market but still aware of me.

I reach into my tote bag for my camera. I can't resist.

"Take one of me," I say, lifting the camera and angling it just right. He snaps it, and I can't stop laughing at the serious concentration on his face.

"Now—one of us together," I add, catching the attention of a vendor nearby. The woman chuckles but obliges, adjusting the lens just so. Beau and I huddle, arms around each other. I grab the camera, then quickly slide it back into my tote bag, grinning at him.

"Perfect," I murmur, my voice soft.

We keep walking, the market alive around us, when something burly and squat catches my eye. My eyebrows shoot up.

"Winnie?" I whisper, incredulous. The pig snorts and squeals, circling a small mound of hay. My mind darts to the remains of the picnic mishap, Winnie eating the leftovers, and tearing around the flower farm.

Harold stands nearby, arms crossed, face tight. "She gets bought today, or she's bacon," he says, voice gruff, but there's a hint of amusement—like he's daring me to try.

Without hesitation, I rip open my tote and dump every bill from the flower stand into his palm.

Beau's hand clamps around my wrist. My heart jumps. I tense, thinking he might stop me, but instead he just holds me there, steady, before turning back to Harold, planting his feet, voice firm.

"The only way you're getting this deal is if you transport that deep litter barn to her property. No barn, no pig. Otherwise, she stays with you—and trust me, she'll outsmart you before breakfast."

Harold huffs, muttering under his breath. But he glances at the excited little pig, pawing at the fence and squealing, and finally relents.

"Fine. Barn goes with her. Happy?"

Winnie snorts, squeals, and trots toward me like she knows she's finally won. I point a finger at her, and for a moment, she pauses, ears twitching, like she's acknowledging she belongs to me.

I peek over at Beau, still holding my wrist, and see that faint twitch of a smile on his lips. My chin lifts with triumph and pure, ridiculous joy. I feel invincible.

Beau

IT'S YOUR LOVE

It's been a few weeks since Hazel's first farmers market. Fall has been creeping over Maple Hollow, and the mornings carry that crisp bite that makes the orchard smell like apples and wood smoke. Leaves swirl along the edges of the paths, some clinging stubbornly to branches, others drifting down to form little golden piles.

Pressed against the barn, boots sinking into the soft dirt, my eyes follow her as she weaves through the greenhouse. She's humming softly, her hands buried in the soil, rearranging seedlings and adjusting the watering cans she insists on carrying herself. Winnie snuffles around her ankles, rooting in the loose soil with that ridiculous sense of ownership only pigs seem to have. Hazel shoots the pig an exaggerated glare, then laughs, shaking her head. I can't help but grin.

The world has slowed into this rhythm, this easy cadence of work, quiet mornings, and small triumphs. I've been helping her prep the greenhouse, haul heavier things, set up supports for climbing plants, but mostly I just watch her find her way, letting her take the lead even when it means she's making mistakes I'd fix in a second. It's satisfying. Seeing her bloom here—literally and figuratively—is better than anything I could have imagined.

I stroll over, brushing a leaf off my shoulder, and she looks up, eyes sparkling, dirt smudged across her fingers and cheeks.

"Morning," I say, voice low. She smiles like I just told the best joke in the world.

"Morning!" She wipes her hands on her apron. "I was just about to start setting up the cold frames. Wanna help?"

I shake my head. "Nah. You've got this."

She does, and I know it. But I linger anyway, near the frame of the greenhouse door, enjoying the way she moves, the way her focus is absolute. It's contagious.

Winnie lets out a loud squeal, plopping herself down in the dirt, completely unbothered by the early chill. Hazel bends down to scratch her behind the ears.

"You're not going to let her run your greenhouse, are you?"

She smirks without looking up. "I've survived worse than a pig who thinks she owns the place."

I can't argue with that.

I give Hazel a smile, the kind that doesn't need words, and she nods back, eyes lighting up.

"I'll be here if you need me," I say, before heading to the orchard.

The greenhouse door shuts softly behind me, leaving her humming to herself over the seedlings. I take a deep breath of crisp fall air, the tang of fallen leaves and ripening apples filling my lungs. The orchard waits, and it's calling me. U-pick season is just around the corner, and there's still plenty to prep before the first visitors arrive.

I start with the pathways, raking leaves that have already begun to carpet the rows. The ground out here is firmer beneath my boots, but the morning frost has left its bite. I grunt as I lift a crate of baskets for picking, muscles tight, joints complaining like old machinery, but I push it aside. This work feels necessary, grounding. Hazel's energy will carry the greenhouse. Mine will carry the orchard.

Next, I check the apple trees, scanning for any signs of rot or early frost damage. A few branches need pruning, and I carefully cut them away, feeling okay with it not being perfect.

The U-pick signs need updating, so I pull out the stack I keep in the shed. I scrawl the dates and times, making a mental note to have the entry gate cleared and the payment box ready. The orchard has always been my Pa's pride, and now, in some ways, it's mine to protect, to manage, to invite others into.

By the time I step back, feeling the day settle into my shoulders, the orchard is coming together beautifully for visitors. The apples shine in the filtered light, the baskets stacked neatly, paths cleared. I step back for a moment, hands on my hips, body feeling heavy but satisfied.

The farmhouse door swings open behind me, Hazel stepping out with a fresh cup of tea, setting it on the step, spotting me in the orchard.

"Hey," she calls, voice light, teasing. "You working me out of a job here?"

I chuckle, wiping dirt from my hands. "Not a chance. You're the boss of the greenhouse. I'm just making sure the orchard doesn't fall apart while you're planting flowers like a madwoman."

She laughs, and I feel it again—the warmth that comes from watching her thrive.

My joints in my hands are stiff, the ache humming under the surface. Hazel doesn't need me whole. She just needs me to be here. Steady. Reliable. Ready for whatever autumn—and she—throw my way.

I catch Hazel's wrist gently, guiding her to the first tree.

"See these apples?" I point to a cluster low on the branch. "You want firm, a little give, and no bruises. Check the stem, too—it should snap clean if it's ready."

She crouches slightly, fingers brushing the fruit, eyes focused but curious. "Like this?"

"Exactly."

Her hand moves over the apple, careful, almost reverent. Her attention to detail makes me smile.

We move down the row, tree by tree, me explaining, her listening, touching, learning. I show her how to twist the fruit just right, how to tell if the color and firmness are perfect. She mimics my motions, her face lighting up each time she gets it right. She's quick, and I can't help but be impressed—and a little distracted by her beauty.

By the time we reach the old apple tree at the back of the orchard—my favorite—I stop. Hazel's looking at me, the grin spreading across her face making my heart thump more than it should. Without a word, I step closer, wrapping my arms around her waist.

She pauses, tense for an instant, then eases herself into me.

My mouth finds hers, and the orchard around us fades away. It's soft, hesitant at first, then deeper, more urgent. Her hands tangle in my shirt, and I hold her tight, feeling the warmth of her, the thrill of this quiet moment we've been dancing around.

When we pull back, she rests her forehead against mine, breath shaky but eyes shining.

"I've never seen you like this," she says softly. "So . . . happy."

I brush a stray lock of hair from her face. "It's your love," I admit, letting the words linger between us.

It's her love.

Hazel

HOME IS HERE

I cradle the phone between my shoulder and ear, balancing a mug of lukewarm tea in my other hand.

"Mom, you wouldn't believe the last month I've had." I am grinning despite myself. "The farmers market was a success. I sold out of every bouquet I brought. People were so welcoming, and—I don't know—it just felt like I belonged there. The fall season is rolling in here, and oh my gosh, the colors, Mom! *The colors!*"

There's a pause on the other end, then her voice, a mixture of disbelief and amusement. "And let me guess . . . you haven't thought about the job offer?"

"I bought a pig."

"*What?!*" There's a sharp, incredulous laugh.

I can't help but laugh, too, shaking my head. "The one that terrorized my picnic leftovers! That exact one. Winnie. And honestly? I think she's already part of the family."

My mom snorts, clearly torn between shaking her head and laughing.

"Hazel, only you could turn a pig rampage into a life lesson and a new family member."

I press my lips together to hide my smile, thinking about

how right this feels—this chaos, this little patch of home, this sense of grounding I never had in my old life.

"It's perfect, Mom. It's messy, but it's mine. And somehow, that makes all the difference."

There's a pause. Then her voice lowers. "Hazel, this is your chance to come back. To be the person you worked so hard to become."

I close my eyes, pressing my fingers into the ceramic of my mug. "But, Mom, that's the thing. I don't want to be her anymore." My voice steadies, surprising even me. "This—this place, these people, this work—it's not a phase. It's where I'm supposed to be."

Silence stretches between us, filled only by the distant sound of a rooster crowing.

"You sound . . . certain."

"I am. It's not perfect, but it's mine. I feel like I'm not just surviving—I'm living. Truly living. And I think I found a really good thing here, a really good *someone*."

A long silence stretches across the line, and then, finally, she says, softer, almost grudgingly, "Well, I can't argue with being happy. Just promise me you'll take care of yourself."

"I will, Mom." Relief easing through me. "You'll get pictures of the pig, the greenhouse, the flowers, every little thing. I promise."

We say our goodbyes, and I hang up, taking a slow breath. My gaze drifts to the fridge, landing on the photograph of Beau and me from the farmers market. My chest swells a little.

Then I notice his muddy boots tucked neatly by the back door, the flannel draped over the breakfast bar, a spare set of his keys sitting on the counter as though he'd just slipped out for a moment. A wave of something—belonging, relief, warmth—washes over me.

This is home.

I look back and forth between my little farmhouse, the cozy chaos I've made of it, and the presence of him threaded through it all. His home has bled into mine in the quietest, sweetest ways. The scent of flannel, the weight of his boots by the door, the memory of his hands lifting me through flower beds.

All of this—it's home.

I didn't give up.

I'm bent over, tugging at Winnie's little legs, trying to coax her out of the narrow space between the couch and the bookcase, going on about "stubborn pigs and their impeccable timing," when I hear a noise behind me.

I freeze, ears straining, thinking maybe it's just the vent kicking on again—or that one floorboard is groaning like it always does. But no. It's a different sound, heavier, deliberate. My head pops up just in time to see that the couch has been pushed back just enough to make space in the middle of the floor. A soft blanket is spread out, cushions tossed around haphazardly, like someone did it in a rush but still cared about comfort.

And then I notice the little wicker basket sitting in the center, the lid slightly askew. My hands freeze mid-motion, still brushing Winnie's back. "Beau . . ." I whisper.

He steps into view from the kitchen, holding a mug of steaming cider.

"Hi," he says, voice casual, but I catch the twinkle in his eye. He sets the mug down carefully on the edge of the blanket. "Thought we'd do a little indoor picnic. Weather's been unpredictable, and you've been working yourself ragged."

I blink, completely disarmed. My mouth opens, then closes, then opens again. "You . . . you did all this?"

He shrugs, like it's nothing, but his smirk betrays him. "You said you wanted to try something new. I figured we could start small."

I'm trying to process it, still tangled between excitement and disbelief. Winnie, oblivious, has made her way into the room and is now circling the blanket, snuffling at the vent, utterly entertained by the odd hissing sound. I can't help but laugh.

Beau crouches down to scratch behind her ears, and the way he moves—gentle and careful—like he's handling something precious, makes my heart stumble in a way that feels entirely new, entirely dangerous.

"C'mon." He pats the blanket beside him. "Sit before you fall over trying to wrangle the chaos. I know we have a stern 'no Winnie in the house' rule, but we can break it this *once*."

I step carefully onto the blanket, taking in every detail—the warm textures of the fabric, the mugs of cider, a small plate of apple crumble, a tiny stack of grilled cheese and extra-crispy fries, and, tucked in a paper bag, his usual burger. All of it smells amazing. Comforting. Perfect.

We settle down, Winnie contentedly snorting around us, occasionally nosing a cushion as if claiming her spot. I sit cross-legged, careful not to spill anything. Beau pours the cider into our mugs. I take a cautious sip—and my eyes widen.

"Oh my gosh," I breathe. "I've never had fresh cider like this . . . it's . . . it's bursting with flavor."

He chuckles softly, sitting back, smiling at me. "Told you it'd be good. First batch of the season." He sips his own. "But it's not just the cider, it's you. You made it worth brewing."

"You're ridiculous," I tease with a smile, shifting a little closer. "But . . . thank you."

We dig into the apple crumble, sharing bites, laughing when Winnie tries to sneak a nibble, and trading stories over grilled cheese and fries. Beau's burger sits there untouched at first, but he eventually digs in, shaking his head at me like I should've warned him about the chaos.

Everything feels slow and perfect, the kind of moment you want to stretch into forever.

The conversation meanders, soft laughter, shared stories about the orchard, the market, little confessions tucked between bites. I catch him smiling more than usual, the kind of soft, contented smile. And somehow, even in this chaos, this mess of a living room turned picnic spot, I feel so . . . loved.

Winnie finally settles beside us, snoring lightly, and I rest against Beau, shoulder to shoulder. He wraps an arm around me, pulling me closer. I take a long, deep breath, savoring the warmth of cider, crumbs, laughter, and the steady beat of his presence beside me.

I peer down at our mugs, at the mess of food and blankets, at Winnie snuggled up like she owns the world, and then I look at Beau. A thought sneaks in without permission. This—this chaotic, imperfect, perfectly ours chaos—is exactly where I'm supposed to be.

And I know, without a doubt, that nothing else—no job offer, no old life, no hesitation—could ever compare to this.

Beau

SEASONS TURNED, YEARS PASSED...

The rooster's already crowing when I roll out of bed, though truth be told, I was awake before him. My body doesn't let me sleep past dawn anymore, not with the way my knees creak and my shoulders stiffen if I stay still too long. Used to be, I cursed it. These days, I take it as my cue to start moving. The farm doesn't wait, and neither do the aches.

I step out onto the porch, mug of black coffee in my hand, and breathe deep. The air is sharp with the kind of coolness only fall mornings carry—like a warning of frost not far off—but underneath it all is the sweet tang of apples and damp earth. The fields stretch out before me, and for a moment I just stand there, letting it sink in.

It's not the same farm it was years ago. Back then, it felt tired, half forgotten, clinging on like I was. Now it's alive. Hazel's flower rows sweep out in tidy stripes of color, even this late in the season—rust-red mums, golden marigolds, purple asters all burning bright against the gray sky. Beyond them, the greenhouse she all but willed into existence glows faintly, fogged windows catching the morning light.

And the orchard stands steady, trees heavy with fruit. The younger ones we planted together are taller now, filling in the gaps between the old gnarled giants I've always favored. Chickens chatter and scratch under the branches, a couple of goats bleating from the pen we built after Hazel decided "a farm needs more voices." She was right. I'd never admit it out loud, but I like the company.

Seems like everything around here is aging. Winnie's much older now, and even Clover—though we got her young—has filled out and settled some. Seasons have passed with her, too. Still, she's the younger, louder, twice-as-stubborn one. The dog's the one I insisted on—an old hound, Maisy, with more patience than either of us. She pads up beside me now and settles at my feet, head resting heavily against my boot.

I take another sip of coffee, scanning the land, listening. It used to be quiet out here, the kind of quiet that gnawed at me. Now it's different. There's life in it. The sound of Hazel humming somewhere down the flower rows. The scrape of a rake from the orchard—Caleb, the young hand who helps me keep up these days. The low whinny of the mare Hazel begged me to buy her for the festivals. I thought it was ridiculous then. Seeing kids line up to pet her every weekend now, I know it wasn't.

My aching body steadies on the porch rail, and I let out a slow breath. The aches are still here. The orchard still asks more of me than I sometimes want to give. But the weight I carry doesn't feel like it used to. This place isn't just survival anymore. It's growth. It's steady. It's ours.

And it's Hazel's laugh, carried across the fields on the morning air, that makes me smile before I even realize I'm doing it.

By midday, the farm is buzzing the way it always does this time of year. The sun's high enough now to burn the frost off the grass, and everything smells alive—apples warming in the light, soil turning under boots, and the faint sweetness of flowers Hazel swears are still in bloom "just because they love us."

Caleb's already in the orchard, stacking the picking baskets I left by the shed earlier. Kid's taller than me now, though he'll always be "the kid" in my mind. He wipes sweat from his brow with the back of his arm, grinning when he spots me.

"Morning, boss," he calls.

I grunt, a greeting laced with humor. "Didn't I tell you not to over stack those? You'll split the slats."

He flashes me that crooked grin. "You always say that, and they never split."

"Because I fix 'em before you notice," I smirk into my coffee cup, hiding the way my chest tugs with a kind of pride I don't want him catching me in. Caleb started out as a scrawny teen looking for odd jobs. Now he's damn near running half the orchard on his own.

Hazel wanders over from the greenhouse, wiping her hands on her apron, dirt smudged along her cheek like she painted it there herself. She's holding a clipboard covered in lists only she can make sense of.

"Did you remind Caleb about the festival crates?" she asks, voice light but edged with that focus she gets when she's in "flower boss" mode.

Caleb grunts, throwing his head back. "Yes, Hazel. Already labeled and stacked. I'm not twelve anymore."

"You'll always be twelve to me." Hazel laughs.

I snort into my coffee, and Caleb shoots me a look. "Don't you start, Beau."

Hazel catches my eye, that mischievous glint in hers, the one that still manages to undo me after all these years. She doesn't say anything, but her smile is enough to remind me we've built all of this together. The orchard. The flowers. Even the ragtag team that now makes Pine & Petal more than just a farm—it's a home.

A squeal cuts across the air, sharp enough to make us all turn. Clover the pig barrels through Hazel's flowers, scattering petals like confetti, with Maisy, the hound, hot on her heels.

"Not again!" Hazel huffs, before sprinting after them, apron flapping, hair catching the light like fire.

Caleb doubles over laughing, hands on his knees. I just shake my head, biting back a smile as I set my cup on the fence post.

"Some farm," I mutter, though the truth is, I wouldn't trade this chaos for anything.

By the time Hazel rounds up Clover—half covered in petals and scolding the pig like it's a wayward toddler—Caleb and I are both pretending to work. She shoots us a glare sharp enough to cut steel, but her lips twitch, betraying her.

"Don't you dare laugh." She points at me.

"Wouldn't dream of it." I lift my hands in surrender, but the grin still creeps across my face.

Her eyes linger on me a moment too long, softening, before she shakes her head. "You two are impossible."

She heads back toward the greenhouse, jokingly cursing under her breath.

"She's gonna get you back for that." Caleb chuckles.

"Yeah," I say, grabbing a basket, testing its weight. "Worth it."

I let the fence post support me once Caleb heads off toward the shed, the orchard quieting down around me. My eyes aren't on the apples anymore. They're on the little band worn smooth by time slipped on my finger. I turn it, slow, like I've done a thousand times. Funny how something so simple can carry the weight of a whole life.

Hazel still wears hers, too. Every so often, I'll catch her fiddling with it, absentmindedly, when she's lost in thought over seedlings or invoices.

My chest tightens when I think back to that day—the way she walked down the path between the orchard and greenhouse, warmth rising in her wake as if the world was trying to keep up with her brightness. She insisted on keeping it here, right where the two worlds touched.

"Between yours and mine," she said, eyes daring me to argue. I didn't. I never could with her.

The animals were everywhere, of course. Winnie trotted ahead like the flower girl, Clover tried to steal bouquets from the baskets, and Maisy barked her approval loud enough to scare off the crows. Folks from town lined the rows, their laughter mixing with the rustle of leaves overhead. No big church, no polished ballroom—just dirt underfoot, blossoms overhead, and the place we made ours.

I remember the way my hands shook when I slipped that simple band on her finger, promising her I'd keep showing up, even on the bad days, even when my body fought me harder than the weather did. She whispered something back, voice steady, eyes clear as ever, *"I never give up."*

She meant it. And every day since, she's proved it.

I twist the band again, the memory sitting heavy and light all at once. Heavy because it still knocks the breath out of me, how much I love her. Light because—hell—I got lucky. I never thought I'd have this. A woman who sees past the mask. A life that's noisy and messy and so full it aches sometimes.

The orchard wind picks up, carrying the scent of apples and hay, and I swear I can still hear her laugh from that day—wild and free, carried up into the trees. It rattles around inside me, softening all the rough edges.

I glance up from the orchard path just in time to see her—Hazel—darting between the rows of wildflowers and apple trees, her strawberry-blonde waves catch the sun like polished amber. She's laughing, chasing after Winnie and Clover, who've apparently decided to stage some kind of miniature rebellion against the new fence. Her arms are full of scraps of ribbon she's clearly been using to mark the rows for next week's planting, and for a second, I just take it all in.

She notices me then, freezes mid-run, and a grin spreads across her face so wide it's practically audible. Her feet pick up speed again, and she comes straight toward me, weaving around the crates and baskets like she's been training for this exact moment. Winnie snorts in her wake, Clover snuffles along, and the entire scene—the messy, chaotic life we've built—feels impossibly perfect.

When she reaches me, she throws her arms around my neck, and I catch her with ease, though my body protests just a little. Her forehead presses to mine, breath warm against my face, and I see her eyes—bright, unguarded, utterly hers. She lifts a hand to my cheek and mouths something.

I freeze for a heartbeat, then the words settle into my chest like they were always meant to be there. *I love you.*

I don't speak. I just mouth it back, letting the words stretch between us, silent but louder than anything I could say aloud.

She laughs softly against my shoulder, the kind of laugh that carries every memory we've made, every late night planning the market, every chaotic morning with the animals, every tender, frustrating, wonderful moment. I brush a hand through her hair, pull her close, and for a moment, I let myself just *be* here, in this life, in this orchard, in this love.

I press a kiss to the top of her head, whispering against her hair, "Mine. Always mine."

She smiles, tilting her head up just enough to catch my eyes, and I can feel the certainty radiating from her as strongly as my own. We don't need words. We don't need a crowd or a stage. This is ours. Right here, right now, forever starting.

And as we stand together, arms wrapped tight, the orchard alive with autumn scent, rustling leaves, and the quiet hum of our home, I know my forever has never looked better.

Hazel's Journal

A PIECE OF FOREVER

Today, the world feels like it's leaning in just for us. Sunlight spills across the orchard, golden and warm, scattering through the leaves and turning every apple into a tiny jewel. I can hear the gentle hum of bees around the wildflowers, Winnie snuffling happily somewhere nearby, and Maisy wagging her tail as if she knows this day is special.

Beau looks ridiculous in the best possible way—his tie slightly crooked, sleeves rolled up like he's ready to work the fields at a moment's notice, but the way his eyes find mine makes every imperfection disappear. I could have been nervous, overwhelmed, terrified that this life, this love, might not feel as real as it does in my dreams—but the minute I stepped into the aisle, framed by our flowers and our farm, it all made sense.

Our vows were messy, a little unpolished, just like the orchard and the greenhouse—but perfect because they were ours. He promised me forever, right here, in the middle of our worlds colliding, with the scent of apples and sun-warmed soil around us. I promised to bug him every lifetime, because some things are worth holding onto forever.

I look around and see our friends, our family, and somehow the animals, too, gathered in our little patch of paradise. It's wild, colorful, a little unpredictable, but it takes root and grows stronger every day, just like the wildflowers in our fields.

Today, I am exactly where I belong. With Beau. With this farm. With the messy, beautiful, sprawling, laughter-filled life we've built together. And yes . . . love blooms here. Wild and true, in every petal, every leaf, every heartbeat.

I have to go now, forever is waiting.

Hazel Rosewood

Low Energy Artisan Bread

For those who suffer low-spoon days

Ingredients:

- 3 cups bread flour
  - 1 1/2 tsp salt
  - 1/2 tsp active dry yeast
  - 1 1/2 cups warm water (105-112 degrees fahrenheit)

Instructions:

1. Mix Gently: In a large bowl, whisk together the bread flour, salt, and yeast. Pour in the warm water and stir with a wooden spoon until just combined. It will look shaggy and sticky —perfect.

    2. Cover and Rest: Cover the bowl with a clean towel or wrap. Let it rest for 6 to 24 hours at room temperature, depending on your spoons and schedule. The dough should double in size and form soft bubbles along the surface, like it's quietly waking up.

    3. First Shape: When it's ready, gently turn the dough out

onto a floured surface. Loosely shape it into a round shape-don't worry about perfection. Let it rest for another 30 minutes, covered lightly.

4. Preheat with Intention: While the dough proofs, preheat your oven to 450°F. Place your baking pans inside to heat up-glass, cast iron, whatever you have WHILE preheating. If you're mimicking steam, set a metal pan on the bottom rack for later ice cubes. (I don't usually mimic steam)

5. Final Shape & Score: After proofing, gently shape the dough once more. Carefully place it into the hot pan. Score the top with a sharp knife or blade—a simple line is enough. This is where it opens up and blooms.

6. Bake with Care: Cover your pan (foil works if you don't have a lid) and bake for 30 minutes. Then remove the cover and bake for an additional 15 minutes, until the crust is golden and crackly, and it sounds hollow when tapped.

7. Cool & Savor: Let the bread cool if you can resist. Once cooled, cut into it and spread with something sweet, and remind yourself: you made this on a hard day. That matters.

Author's Note:

This recipe was made with gentle days in mind—those moments when chronic pain or fatigue make everything feel heavier. As someone who also walks that path yet still finds comfort in the rhythm of homemade bread, I hope this brings you ease, nourishment, and a little love with every bite.

Rosewood Cinnamon Apples

Inspired by Where Wildflowers Bloom

Ingredients:

- 7–8 apples, peeled and sliced
    - 1/2 cup granulated sugar
    - 1/4 cup packed brown sugar
    - 1 tablespoon cinnamon (measure with your heart)
    - 3 tablespoons cornstarch
    - 2 tablespoons butter, cubed
    - A splash (or more) of vanilla extract

Instructions:

1. Prepare the apples: Peel and slice the apples, then place them into the bowl of your crockpot.
    2. Combine the ingredients: Add the sugar, brown sugar, cinnamon, cornstarch, and vanilla extract. Stir well to coat the apples evenly.
    3. Add the butter: Scatter the cubed butter over the top of the apple mixture.

4. Cook: Cover and cook on high for 2–3 hours, or until the apples are tender and the sauce has thickened.

5. Serve warm over ice cream, pancakes, or enjoy straight from the bowl for a cozy treat.

Author's Note:

This recipe was created with Beau in mind, a quiet nod to his life among the rows of apple trees, where each season tells its own story. I like to imagine him stirring a batch of these cinnamon apples after a long day in the orchard, letting the sweetness of tradition fill his kitchen.

Playlist

SHAKE THE FROST (LIVE) - TYLER CHILDERS

Call Your Mom - **Noah Kahan**
Redwoods - **Haley Heynderickx**
Vienna - **The Army, The Navy**
Mouth of a Flower - **Haley Heynderickx**

Keep reading for a sample of Beyond the Teacups

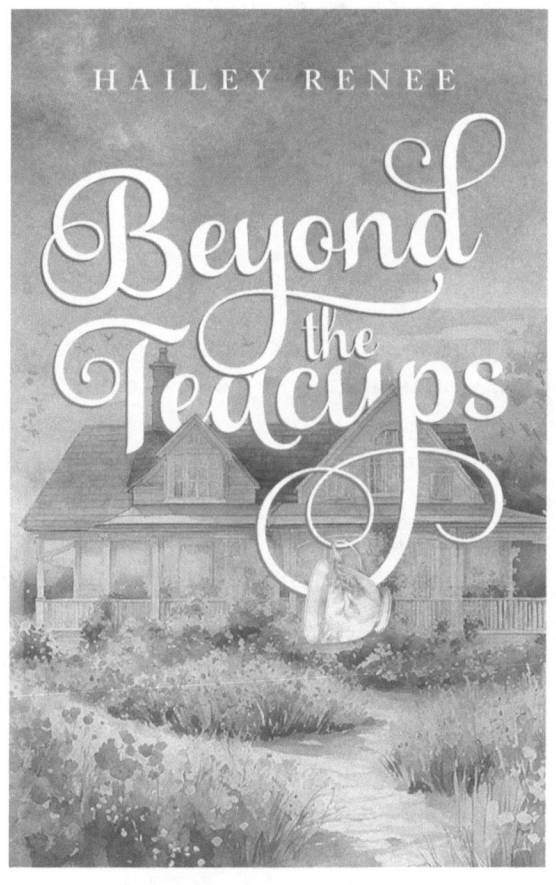

*Part of the
The Homegrown Hearts
Collection*

A Sip Before

BEYOND THE TEACUPS

The rich aroma of pumpkin and chocolate wafts through the air, wrapping me in a familiar embrace. My hands move without thinking, instinct guiding me as I scoop the thick pumpkin mixture into perfect cookies, their soft, warm texture beneath my fingertips. It's a routine as old as the walls of this house—mix, bake, display, repeat.

Add the constant rhythm of tea brewing, kettles filling, and clinking teacups. The kitchen is eerily quiet today, except for the gentle crinkling of parchment as I slide freshly baked cookies onto it. I take in this moment's warmth and sweet comfort, letting it settle around me. Yet, as I begin to put the cooled cookies into small brown paper bags, I can't shake the weight of something pressing down on me . . .

A restlessness, a question, something that returns repeatedly, like a whisper carried on the wind. I glance around at the renovated first floor of my childhood home, now a beautiful tea and bakery shop. The mismatched teacups, the old wooden beams, the shelves filled with jars of tea, spices, and little trinkets—it's all mine. Every corner of this place is shaped by my hands, my heart. But . . . is this it?

Is this all there will ever be?

"What if everything changes?" The words slip from my lips, barely more than a breath. I pause, staring down at the row of neatly packed cookies. My voice sounds strange and foreign, as if it belongs to someone else. "What if there really is more than this?"

The thought lingers in the air, both unsettling and exhilarating.

I did not welcome the change.

Ophelia

BEYOND THE TEACUPS

Music floods from the record player in the corner of the room, wrapping me in its melody. Something about a good tune really sets the mood.

My wooden worktable has a patchwork of small bowls scattered about, filled with dried herbs and fragrant tea leaves. The comforting smell of chamomile mingles with the sharper, citrusy zest of the dried orange peels—a combination I have been toying with for a few weeks.

Today, I'm determined to get it just right. I add a pinch of lemon balm for a mild, soothing undertone and just the faintest sprinkle of dried hibiscus to blend the color once steeped. I am excited. This looks stunning already. As I work, the rhythm of my movements has my skirt twirling around my legs. I try to ignore the tiny swats from my one-eyed cat, dashing back and forth. Nothing was going to stop me from perfecting this blend today.

The kettle whistles, pulling me from my thoughts. I reach for a teacup off the wooden shelf and filled it with hot water. The dried ingredients began to unfurl and tint the liquid a soft peach. The scent wafting up was delicate but intriguing—a hint of citrus blanched by the mellow sweetness of chamomile.

I hold the cup, inhaling the deepest breath before taking the first sip. Warmth spreads through me as the flavors dance on my tongue. It wasn't perfect, not yet, but it was close. I grab my journal and jot down a quick note:

Chamomile and orange peel base.

Needs a touch more . . . brightness? Maybe some mint?

I paused, tapping the pen against my lips. The music still envelops my soul in peace as I clean up a few of the messy areas of my work table before preparing myself for yet another round of trial and error with this blend.

It is so close to being perfect. I reach for another scoop of chamomile when my music abruptly stops. I'm stunned back into reality, suddenly aware of the thundering crashes in my chest as my heart rate quickens.

I look at my wristwatch. It's still two hours before the teahouse opens to the townsfolk, but I did leave the front door unlocked in case any of the homeschool co-ops wanted to spend their early morning sessions enjoying some free baked goods reheated from last night's run.

I turn into the main room, but nothing prepares me for the impending doom in the corner—Emmett Sterling.

"Did someone order mail?" Emmett says in an icy voice.

I look at his hands, praying to anyone who would listen that a package would accompany the letters, but no. He holds a singular pink envelope.

"Are all mailmen this invasive?" I ask, shooting him a look, though the racing in my chest is not letting up, and my fingers feel tingly.

"Only the good-looking ones." He winks.

I coach myself through the want-to-gag, but he catches my hunch.

"Ophelia Mossgrove, are you repulsed?" He huffs as he tosses the envelope on a nearby table.

I hesitate but ultimately go through the sea of chairs to get it. *Wool & Whisker's Vet Services* was in bold on the front. I process this before doing something I wouldn't normally consider—I send the envelope flying into the man before me, and it hits his chest with a pathetic thump before delicately falling to the ground.

My eyes widen as I realize I just assaulted the mailman. Well, Emmett Sterling who happens to be the mailman, but still.

"Did you just throw mail at me?" He bends to grab the letter on the floor.

I don't answer. I have an anxiety attack on speed dial and a tea blend that needs perfecting. Emmett would not get the best of me today, but the replies were loading in my head on autopilot.

He smiles. "Oh, I see, reverting to the cottage in your head to avoid the charming man in front of you?"

My cheeks flush pink before I twirl around, a last-ditch effort to stick it to him. With all the emotion I can muster, I whip my head back and spit out, "You can't even deliver mail correctly. Nothing about you is charming,"

With that, I disappear back into the kitchen. My heart feels like it's making its way up my throat, my eyes pulse, and my fingers tingle. Something about that man makes me feel so angry, but maybe it was because I have been dealing with him and his inability to deliver mail correctly for the past five months. I need the package he claims was lost, but I know he misdelivered it, and someone is bound to return it to the post office.

At least, that is what I keep hoping for. I look at my watch again—an hour and a half before opening.

Perfect. I could spend another half hour on the blend and then an hour prepping for opening. I am so thankful I woke up as early as I did. Getting ready before the sun came out was never fun, but having my mornings to myself really fulfills my soul. It wouldn't be too long before the rare lull of this silence was replaced with the bustling sounds of townsfolk and their all-too-familiar orders.

I peek around the corner once more. The spot where Emmett once stood is now empty. I hear the rumble of his truck exiting the gravel driveway. *Thank God.* I twirl around and replace the silence with music as I dance my way back to the kitchen, humming and returning to the rhythmic adventure that was tea making.

Okay, let's do this . . . *again.* I reach for another scoop of chamomile, the same amount of orange peels, a dash of lemon balm, and a whisper of mint. My fingers trace the bowl's rim as if sealing the moment into memory. *Let's see if you are as perfect as you look.*

I add more water to the kettle and adjust the knob as I inspect the flame to put it just right. I lean against the counter. Poe is sunbathing in the filtered light cascading from the back door window.

I have so much to do as the fall season rolls in. Decorating, curating a new menu, decluttering the storage room, and my least favorite task . . . an oil change for my sweet Chevy, which is bunkered out there in the impending cold. The hum of the kettle blankets my nerves like an encouraging friend. I fill the teacup once again with hot water. The steam curls upward, the scent blooming thicker than last time. The water expanded with a golden hue kissed with pink.

The cup's warmth spreads through my palms, and I let my lips land on the rim, slowly sipping the liquid. Bright, gentle, inviting—the aroma is divine. I set the cup down, vibrating with excitement. I scoop Poe up and hold him high in the air. "*We did it! That's it!*"

I did it, but he was the emotional support I needed. I look around, eyeing my notebook before jotting down several almost unreadable words: *Name: Haven's Bloom.*

I toss the pen on the counter. Now, we need to make a few dozen muffins . . .

Acknowledgments

Before you close this book, I'd like a moment, not author to reader, but soul to soul.

Writing Beau was both easy and hard. His gruffness felt familiar, yet sometimes difficult to sit with. His joint pain mirrored my own flares, and his fear of naming it was my lived experience.

If you—or someone you love—navigate chronic pain, please know this: you are seen, in the good, the hard, and everything in between.

And now, for the personal hugs: little pieces of my heart sent your way, which I hope you'll take in if you read them.

I want to express my love and gratitude to Amanda Ellenburg, Julie Pilat, and Destiney Calman for lending their magic in naming some of these dear characters—Maggie, Saffron, and Melody. You three hold a special place in my heart, and now, thanks to you, a piece of your magic lives forever on these pages.

I would also love to highlight and celebrate my cover artist and line editor, Brittany Padgett—author of The Reeds of West Hills. She has created the covers for the first two books in The Homegrown Hearts Collection, and readers have adored every one of them. Beyond her incredible talent, Brittany is a truly inspiring writer, and I am deeply honored to have her in my corner.

I will spend the rest of my life giving thanks to my mentor, publisher, friend, and inspiration, Brittany Tucker—author of

The Calamities of Camden Callahan and other incredible fantasy works—for her unwavering dedication to nurturing my creativity and for being the most steadfast support a person could ask for. I would not be here without following in the footsteps she blazed before me.

And lastly, Irene Daniels—author of Taviny's Blood series. A friendship covered in ink. A bond woven in words. A gratitude set for life. Thank you for being the quiet anchor in the swirl of socials, the steadfast shoulder, and the loudest cheer when being perceived feels heavy. I know your grandmother is proud.

About the Author

Hailey Renee is the author of *The Homegrown Hearts Collection* —cozy romance novellas stitched with representation for life's overlooked corners. Her stories celebrate small towns, heartfelt connections, and the quiet beauty of everyday life.

Beyond writing, Hailey supports fellow authors as a personal assistant, crafts beauty as a florist, and embraces tradition as a folk practitioner. Whether through words, blooms, or a touch of old-world wisdom, she believes in the power of storytelling to heal, to connect, and to bring a little more love into the world.

Also by Hailey Renee
THE HOMEGROWN HEARTS COLLECTION:

Beyond the Teacups
Where Wildflowers Bloom

www.ingramcontent.com/pod-product-compliance
Lightning Source LLC
LaVergne TN
LVHW041220080526
838199LV00082B/1332